MERCY! NO! HOW? WHY?

JAMES SMITH

Writers Apex

Gateway Towards Success

8063 MADISON AVE #1252
Indianapolis, IN 46227
+13176596889
www.writersapex.com

This book is dedicated
In Loving Memory of Bill Burkett

This book is dedicated not only to the memory of Bill Burkett, but also to the legacy which he has contributed to the teachings and to the admonition for holy living as delivered to us by the Apostles of our Lord Jesus, the Christ of God.

Brother Bill frequently ministered in the church in north Texas of which I was a member, as our pastor and Brother Bill shared a strong binding commitment to holiness as well as to adhering to the injunction of the Apostles doctrine. Many times when Bill came down we would spend many hours loitering through various computer stores as he enjoyed computer technology and I enjoyed building them. Every time I would build a new system I could depend on Bill to distribute the old systems and software to pastors who would be able to use them. Bill would often call me for help when he was having computer problems, and even had me in his home to work on his computers. Just as many others, I have spent much time in fellowship with Bro. Bill over the past 40 some years.

After Bill semi-retired from the mission field, he accepted the pastorate to pioneer a small church in Indiana that was started by a very close pastor friend who had passed away. While there Bill would still call me as he had many times in the past when he was having computer problems. After buying a new computer, Bill called me and asked if I would come set it up or him, as he had a certain way in which he wanted his computers set up. After I assured him I would come Bill asked if I would move up there to help him, especially as he was very concerned about the degeneration of his website. At his bidding along with the deep prodding of the Lord I finally acquiesced to a change of address.

Having moved to Alabama, after the Lord told him his ministry here in Indiana was finished, he again had me to come down to reset his computers for him. The last time I visited him in his home in Alabama, I asked him if he would read a manuscript I was working on, and if he thought it meritorious, to write a forward for it, which he kindly consented to. It was a couple of months after this, that after his last hospital stay, "The Old Warrior": as he called himself, laid down his dented and worn armor as he was received up into glory. I miss you my dear friend and Brother, but I wouldn't have you to come back!

FORWARD

The greatest bible scholars down through ages of church history have differed on the doctrine of the Godhead. In this twenty first century the church is still divided between what we call the Oneness and the Trinitarians. Servitus lost his life for his views when he was executed by being burned at the stake with green wood by Calvin who was then governor of Genva. (1553). To explain the Godhead remains to this day an extremely complex subject with so many schools of thought.

Brother Smith has put together on these pages a fresh attempt to help us understand this doctrine, better he also has managed to help us understand ourselves as a being possessing a trinity, spirit, soul and body and how we relate and react to the calamities we all face in life and how understanding our own Trinitarian make-up we can better cope with those tragedies and trials.

I am sure after reviewing what is written on these pages there is something here to help everyone to have a right concept of our heavenly Father and at the same time help you cultivate a better relationship with God and man.

2 Corinthians 10:5 Casting down imaginations, and every high thing that exalteth itself against the knowledge of God, and bringing into captivity every thought to the obedience of Christ; Colossians 1:10 That ye might walk worthy of the Lord unto all pleasing, being fruitful in every good work, and increasing in the knowledge of God;

2 Peter 1:2 Grace and peace be multiplied unto you through the knowledge of God, and of Jesus our Lord, Missionary evangelist Bill Burkett, Bible teacher, author.

INTRODUCTION

As a baby boomer growing up in the forties and fifties, with this nation emerging from the upheaval resulting from the effects of World War II, there wasn't much questioning God concerning the tragedies and disasters that often occurred, as then they were just an unfortunate fact of life. When they did strike people grieved and prayed with and for those who were affected, and simply helped however and wherever they were able, and life carried on as usual, as they looked to God, their primary source of strength, help, aid and comfort.

During this course of time, faith was strong, and for the vast majority of time faith was the only hope people had, as their dependance on God was vitally crucial for their survival in the tough times this nation was experiencing. At this time, patriotism was strong and united, laws were respected and observed, the family circle was unbroken and respected, and the authority of scripture was the fundamental doctrine and discipline of the church even though there were doctrinal differences among denominations. A court's ruling issued by judges was in accordance to the unchanging principles of established legislated law. Schools were allowed to teach moral values, patriotism, as well as biblical truth. Prayer along with the Pledge of Allegiance was allowed to open a school day, and was a necessity for opening town hall meetings, all council meetings, legislative sessions, as well as sporting events. Catastrophic events and other tragedies brought this nation to its knees seeking God's help and direction, instead of bringing riling accusations against Him.

In the sixties major changes began to take place in this country as satanic devastation began its ruse by wrapping its fierce diabolical tentacles around the pulse of this nation with a death squeeze strangling its moral fiber so that man's depraved nature would not only be the rule of law, but the heart beat of this nation as well. The main theme of popular music at this time was country and western which were ballads or folk songs, portraying a narrative or an epic saga, such as "Tumbling Tumbleweeds," "Cool Water," and "Ghost Rider's in the Sky etc." while in the red light districts bawdy music was the main theme of the dives, bars and honky tonks.

Reeling from the tenacious grip of moral decadence the spiritual temperature of this nation began its decline, as the red light districts became respectable areas of commerce, the era of the ballads and epic saga of country and western music faded, as it were into oblivion while the bawdy music of the honky tonks began emerging in main stream society under the guise of country music. With the fever of the new style of country music on the rise, the carnal lyrics of the bawdy songs took on a sordid disposition of somebody done me wrong wailing songs, or crying in my beer tear jerking songs, and songs extolling marital infidelity.

With music having major sway over the temperament of human emotions, the moral temperature of this nation began to fall, as the fervor of the abject lyrics of the new style of country music weaseled its way into the heart, mind and soul of a major portion of the populace of this nation replacing biblical morality. The standard of morality continued its downward digression as the expressive suggestive lyrics of the base content of this new style of country music became ingrained in the heart and mind of society ushering in a new brand of ethics that are diabolically opposed to those of traditional morale values. The unchaste base content of the lyrics of country music has become the standard code of conduct of a new deviant lifestyle in this nation, as you become what you feed your mind with.

War soon emerged between traditional values and the demand for constitutional rights of amoral behavior that was being demanded by the new morality. This war succeeded in dividing this nation between left-wing and right-wing ideologies. This war is still an on-going conflict delivering this nation into the death grip of political correctness which has diverted it from the biblical straight and narrow way onto the destructive broad way, all the way from the common house to the church house championing the new lifestyle spawned by the suggestive lyrics of country music.

With the change in morality unleashed on society through the sway of the new country music frenzy, the church as well started its downward spiral with an outgrowth of modern music labeled gospel rock. Gospel rock was supposedly a spiritual off-shoot of the rock-n'-roll craze that immersed this nation in teen age rebellion in a worldly attempt to keep rebellious youth in church. The iconoclastic style of gospel rock was designed to enslave the unrestrained lusts of the defiant youth of church going families. Before the onslaught of gospel rock, the church relied on the tenets of sound Biblical doctrine for its relationship with God. It was this relationship along with the aid of the melodious strains of the church orchestra, that congregations entreated the presence of God into their service through prayer and orderly praise and worship of soul and spirit. As the fever of gospel rock became accepted within church, the fervor of worship within the church changed from entreating the presence of God through spirit filled worship, to the worship of the flesh as the ear splitting blasting of syncopated drum blasts, accompanied by the merciless thumping of electric bass guitars took over the song service, driving the hearts of congregants into the mass hysteria of uncultured barbaric frenzy. Singers then had to scream into microphones to be heard above the migraine splitting agitation of the hullabaloo. In the eyes of this pilgrim, this is nothing more than the invitation of heathen worship into the church service! Churches soon split over church officials allowing the permanent implementation of this new degraded form of worship in their service in order to keep from losing their young people who were enamored by the aura of the syncopated beat and the screaming of the youth as well as the screaming of the singers which they experienced at rock concerts. Churches soon died as the older generation left over the decision to keep this new sordid form of music, and the young people fell away as this style of worship cemented their relationship with the wanton world of unbridled cravings and not with the Lord Jesus Christ.

As the squeeze of iniquity continued its tenacious grip not only on this nation, but the entire Christian world, major rejection of the supreme authority of God rose as "Hath God said" spawned a myriad of new bible translations. These translations introduced volumes of modified passages that altered the meaning of the Authorized text. These new varied translations also eliminated entire passages of the Authorized text claiming that the passages omitted from the authorized version were not part of the earlier manuscripts. The basis of these new modern versions were from the Textus Vaticanus derived from the Alexandrian manuscripts, as opposed to the Textus Sinaiticus which is the base of the Authorized version.

The liberal reasoning for these translations, is to make the biblical text understandable to modern man, ignoring the fact that the original text is the mind of God, and that the carnal mind of man is "enmity against God, and is not subject to the law of God:" (Romans 8:7). It was through the carnality of mind that these new versions were contrived. These modern volumes exerts influence on unstable minds attributing to their inability to understand the pure mind of God. This relentless squeezing of the carnal mind has even corrupted many pulpits, as these new versions have been preferred and accepted over, as well as replacing the use of the authorized version in a vast number of churches. Church leadership has found it is easier for the church ministries to conform to the mind of the people instead of teaching and exhorting the people to the discerning of the mind of God through Holy Ghost exhortation and sound Biblical exegesis.

The squeeze continued upon this nation with prayer being ousted from the school house, and no longer being acceptable or allowed in the public sector. The Ten Commandments being replaced with liberal philosophy, laws being legislated by activist judges in an effort to force total allegiance to liberal ideology on the entire populace by circumventing due legalized legislated law. Laws also being enacted so that the only ones who are to be offended or discriminated against are Bible believing Christians, as they are the ones keeping God from being completely eliminated from this nation, and are being deemed as dangerous enemies of the state. Political correctness has resulted in God being issued a "pink slip" and ordered to leave the country by the liberal element of this nation. The impudence of political correctness also demanding that conservatism conform to left wing ideology as holiness is a severe cause of discrimination against the liberal agenda. The persistent iniquitous squeeze of diabolical tentacles continues, with moral justice vastly becoming sin as the rise of political correctness becomes the national standard of holiness replacing moral virtue.

Having been loosed form its moorings by the liberal elements of the church world, moral justice has taken a radical downward spiral as the fervor of this nation plunges to deeper depths of degradation, the same as it was in the days of the judges of Israel, with every man doing what is right in his own eyes. With elements within the church world questioning the biblical authority over sexual orientation, the acceptance of multi-gender status, as well as questioning the ethics of the slaughter of the innocence through abortion, extending dignity to euthanasia, political correctness has become the mantra of liberal church doctrine as denominations debate the acceptance of so-called sins that are condemned by scripture simply due to the lack of inclusion.

Now when disaster strikes, or terrorism invades peace and tranquility, or catastrophes overwhelm us God is habitually called to task as the underlying culprit for such tragedies, as the "sparing of the rod has spoiled the child," and as "the imagination of man's heart is evil from his youth," which only gets worse with age instead of improving. As the morals of this nation have taken a spiral turn southward after issuing the demand for God to leave this nation, government houses, courts, schools, even to being ousted from some church denominations through political correctness, liberal ideology isn't able to provide any politically correct answer as to why cataclysmic events are descending on us as never before, and will continue to befall us. The turmoil of chaotic confusion will continue engulfing this nation as our government has deteriorated from a government of the people, by the people, and for the people, to a battleground between right wing and left wing ideologies. As the political environment of the entire world disintegrates into satanic insanity, I am reminded of what Jesus said, that "these things must come to pass, but the end is not yet."

While as yet an enemy of righteousness, being consumed with hate, lust, greed, sensuality, and even to the destruction of relationships, I was without even one real friend in this world. That is until a man where I worked started dealing with my lack of any spirituality, to whom I constantly laughed at under my breath, every time he would witness to me. That is until I started reading a Bible for myself. Then as I read, I stopped laughing and started listening.

One night as I was sleeping, I found myself suddenly awakened, having been thrown out of bed and lying on the floor with my entire body from the top of my head to the soles of my feet engulfed in paresthesia rendering me barely able to control any bodily movement. As I lay in this condition an heavy evil presence flooded the room enticing me with unlimited total sensual satisfaction of anything I wanted. As I lay there trying to gain a sense of composure, a lighter peaceful presence entered the room urging me to hold steady and not to give in to fulfilling the demands that my body was craving at that time. As I lay there in obedience to the placid aura of the second presence, the heavy chaotic atmosphere of the room became tranquil and light as the first evil presence being forced out left. Later after gaining spiritual understanding I realized that I was in a warfare between Satan and the Lord Jesus Christ and that my body was the battle ground. This encounter soon left me addicted with an insatiable appetite for holiness, which was diametrically opposed to the lying sensual life I had been living.

As I began growing in Christ, a spiritual battle soon began raging within my soul between the commands of the Torah and the demands of the Talmud. In those early years, this conflict as to why God allowed things to happen and why He didn't prevent certain things from happening began raging in my soul as well.

With the violence of liberal legality raging in this nation, the "blame game" is on everything especially the degenerate state of man. Realizing the intensity of the spiritual warfare the church is engaged in, an investigation looking into the source of the deterioration of the moral climate of this nation, as well as within elements of the church world was initiated. Here is report on the results of that investigative examination. This examination is not a defense of God, as God is sovereign and does not need defending by any mortal, however, God demands obedience of His children.

It is through divine help that I was able to complete this investigation as fresh thoughts and ideas kept stirring my mind giving me a deeper insight into the argument.

Liberals versus Conservatives

Conservatives believe that law is established on the supreme authority of unchanging principles and that people are subject to the unchanging principles of law.

Liberals believe that there is no absolute established authority, and that Law should change as people change, and that law is subject to change to conform to the depraved politically correct moral values of man.

OH! NO! HOW?......
WHY?

How could God ......? Why did God ......? Why would God ......? Why doesn't God ......? Where was God ......? Does God care ......? Why can't God ......? How is a loving God ......? Why didn't God ......? Why won't God ......? How can God ......? Why will God ......? Why must God ......?

These are but a few of the many accusations and grievances that are laid against God after innumerable calamities, disasters, tragedies, or catastrophes that plague, cripple, obliterate, mutilate, destroy or annihilate friends, families, nations, and even ourselves, have unleashed their devastation, ravaging nations, communities, even ourselves, bringing us to a point of hopeless despair.

Perhaps the two most flagrant asked questions are, "Why did God create sin in the first place?" and "Why does God allow sin?" At issue, how can a pure holy God, the form of whose purity and holiness is impossible to be beheld by mortal flesh, create anything that would in any way violate or stain the purity of His divine righteous holy character and nature, or create anything that He totally despises and hates, and which He will ultimately condemn? So you reply; Well He did create man didn't He? True, however, man was originally created righteous and was clothed in pure holiness. How could man or anything created by God be anything but pure, as purity is the very essence of God's holy character? However, to answer these two questions as well as to the origin of sin, we need to start with an observation of God Himself.

God being empyreal in nature, is not observable in physical fleshly form. Wherefore when he cometh into the world, he saith, Sacrifice and offering thou wouldest not, but a body hast thou prepared me: Hebrews 10:5. That body being the physical incarnate Christ; Who is the image of the invisible God, the firstborn of every creature: Colossians 1:15. When addressing the unbelief of the religious faction following Him, Jesus cried and said, He that believeth on me, believeth not on me, but on him that sent me. 45 And he that seeth me seeth him that sent me. 46 I am come a light into the world, that whosoever believeth on me should not abide in darkness. John 12:44-46. The incarnate Christ is the corporal image of God.

As God cannot be physically observed by the human eye: And he (God speaking to Moses) said, Thou canst not see my face: for there shall no man see me, and live. Exodus 33:20; we can however, get a good view of God by observing scripture. This dialogue between God and Moses in Exodus 33:20, began in Exodus 3:7, when Moses was on mount Sinai receiving the tables of the law, the ten commandments, the torah, at the hand of God.

Meanwhile, Israel, ignoring or disregarding all of the miracles God performed on their behalf in delivering them from Egyptian bondage, demonstrating for them His power and might, were engaging in the idolatrous worshiping of the golden calf: And the LORD (*Yhovah*[1]) said unto Moses, Go, get thee down; for thy people, which thou broughtest out of the land of Egypt, have corrupted *themselves*: 8 They have turned aside quickly out of the way which I commanded them: they have made them a molten calf, and have worshipped it, and have sacrificed thereunto, and said, These *be* thy gods, O Israel, which have brought thee up out of the land of Egypt. Exodus 32:7-8. LORD in verse 7, is referring to God the Father or *Jehovah*[1], which is the Jewish national name of God[1]. Other Hebrew words used for God are *Eloah*[2] and *Eloheem*[3]. (*Eloah*[2]), the singular form of God, refers to God the Father alone. God the Son and God the Holy Ghost who are co-equal with God the Father, yet being of separate personages of the godhead, are referred to as (*Eloheem*[3]) which is the plural of (*Eloah*[2]) and is used when referring to more than one member of triune godhead, the Father, the Son, and the Holy Ghost. However, (*Eloheem*[3]) is also used at times when referring to God the Father only.

THE ORIGIN OF SIN

The first event to happen was Creation.
And Creation was a direct act of God.

A children's story Bible that I was given began with the words "God was lonely, so He decided to make a world." This is simply not true. God is One God, in three persons eternally. Therefore, there was never a time when God was lonely, and there was never a time when God was not a God of love. The fact that time itself began, when God created, does not mean that He did not exist before there was time. Francis Schaeffer[4] explained it thus:

Something existed before creation and that something was personal and not static; the Father loved the Son; there was a plan; there was communication; and promises were made prior to the creation of the heavens and the earth.

God created the universe for a purpose. While we cannot plumb the depths of every aspect of that purpose, we do receive hints. God's purposes were designed collectively, by the three persons of the Trinity. The Creation was designed to give glory to Him. And our part in the Creation order is only significant, in that God has chosen to glorify Himself through making humanity, and placing us on this planet, to do His will.

Creation was not a random chance act. Nor was it a mindless act, of an open, hands-off God. The Bible shows us that God is in complete control, and His ultimate purposes for this Creation will not be thwarted, because these things were decided before the beginning. https://creationmoments.com/sermons/before-the-beginning/
Copyright © 2019 by Creation Moments, Inc., P.O. Box 839, Foley, MN 56329 or www.creationmoments.com. Used by permission

As noted in Francis Schaeffer's commentary notes, all three members of the godhead were present during the Genesis account of creation.[4]

1. God the Father (Eloheem[3]): And, Thou, Lord (*kurios[5]*), in the beginning hast laid the foundation of the earth; and the heavens are the works of thine hands: 11 They shall perish; but thou remainest; and they all shall wax old as doth a garment; 12 And as a vesture shalt thou fold them up, and they shall be changed: but thou art the same, and thy years shall not fail. Hebrews 1:10-12. Lord in Hebrews 1:10 refers to God, the supreme personage of the godhead.

2. God the Son: In the beginning was the Word, and the Word was with God, and the Word

was God. 2 The same was in the beginning with God. 3 All things were made by him; and without him was not any thing made that was made. John1:1-3. The work of the Word, Jesus, in creation testified to by the Apostle John, is confirmed by the Apostle Paul to the Ephesian church: And to make all *men* see what *is* the fellowship of the mystery, which from the beginning of the world hath been hid in God, who created all things by Jesus Christ: Ephesians 3:9. The Apostle also confirms this to the church at Colosse: For by him (Jesus) were all things created, that are in heaven, and that are in earth, visible and invisible, whether *they be* thrones, or dominions, or principalities, or powers: all things were created by him, and for him: 17 And he is before all things, and by him all things consist. Colossians 1:16-17.

3. God the Holy Spirit, *ruach*[6]: And the earth was without form, and void; and darkness *was* upon the face of the deep. And the Spirit (*ruach*[6]) of God moved (*rachaph*[7]) upon the face of the waters. Genesis 1:2. The Holy Spirit is the silent member of the Godhead. Howbeit when he, the Spirit of truth, is come, he will guide you into all truth: for he shall not speak of himself; but whatsoever he shall hear, *that* shall he speak: and he will shew you things to come. John 16:13. Being the silent constituent of the Godhead, the Holy Ghost is not to be spoken

evil of. Wherefore I say unto you, All manner of sin and blasphemy shall be forgiven unto men: but the blasphemy *against* the *Holy* Ghost shall not be forgiven unto men. Matthew 12:31.

John in his first epistle confirms the trinity: For there are three that bear record in heaven, the Father, the Word, and the Holy Ghost: and these three are one. 1 John 5:7. For an understanding the trinity of the Godhead, see figure1

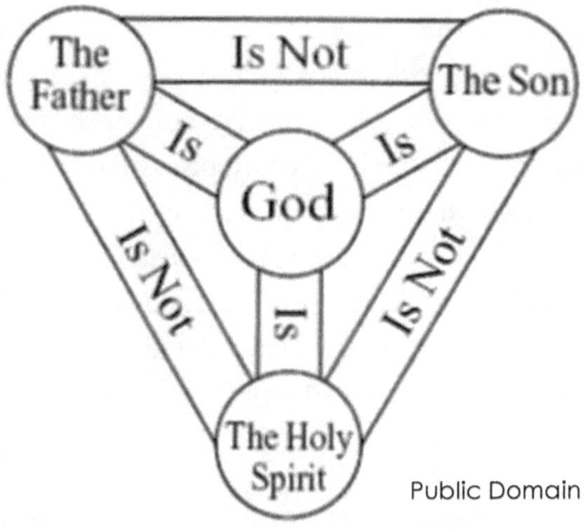

Public Domain

Figure 1 The Triune Godhead

There are several schools of thought concerning the creation narrative presented in the first chapter of Genesis. One thought being that this is the original work of creation. Another view being that this is a restoration of the original creation that had been devastated by a cataclysmic event that occurred sometime after the original creation. One speculation of that cataclysmic event is a war that had been fought between Michael and the holy angels against Satan and his minions at the time of their expulsion from heaven. This being rationalized by the Spirit, (*ruach*[6]), moving (moved *rachaph*[7]) i.e. hovering over the face of the waters, as a mother hen flutters protectively over her brood. This moving of the Spirit, (*ruach*[6]), was as if to survey the carnage the earth was left in as the result of a catastrophic conflict, and that the creation account of Genesis one, is actually a restoration of the original creation of earth. Without any confirming evidence of eternity past, it matters little as to one's view of how creation began. For the prophecy came not in old time by the will of man: but holy men of God spake *as they were* moved by the Holy Ghost. The Biblical record of the Genesis account of creation states that God, (*Eloheem*[3]) still created the heavens and the earth by Christ Jesus. Never the less, from Genesis 1:1-25 the triune godhead (*Eloheem*[3]) was involved in the six day creation.

On day six of creation (*Eloheem*[3]), God the father said: "Let us make man in our image (*tselem*[8]) after our likeness;" Genesis 1:26. The question then is, who is "us" of Genesis 1:26? During this period in earth's history there were only two classes of beings in existence, the eternal Godhead, (*Eloheem*[3]), and the angels who were created by (*Eloheem*[3]). Both classes being empyreal. The "us" could not have been the angels, who themselves were created beings, and were not on an equal with the triune God head, (*Eloheem*[3]) and did not have any known function in creation: But to which of the angels said he at any time, Sit on my right hand, until I make thine enemies thy footstool? Are they not all ministering spirits, sent forth to minister for them who shall be heirs of salvation? Hebrews 1:13-14. The answer can only be God the father, (*Eloah*[2]) that is Lord, (*Eloheem*[3]) the supreme authority of the godhead, addressing the other members that make up the triune Godhead, (*Eloheem*[3]), that is God the Father speaking to God the Son and God the Holy Spirit. See figure 1.

The expression 'Let us make' does not explicitly set forth the doctrine of the Trinity, but it is in keeping with that doctrine."[9] So God created man in his *own* image (*tselem*[8]), in the image of God created he him; male and female created he them. Genesis 1:27. Being made in the image of God does not include physical characteristics. Involved instead are attributes such as intellect, self-consciousness, emotion, self-determination, and the capacity to love, communicate, and have fellowship with God. We might include the capacity to "create," or think independently and originally, as something we share with God.

Being made in God's image also involves a shared authority, by which man is granted rule over the rest of the created order. Man was created to be a ruler; as David wrote, "You made him a little lower than the heavenly beings and crowned him with glory and honor"; 4What is man, that thou art mindful of him?

and the son of man, that thou visitest him?[5] For thou hast made him a little lower than the angels, and hast crowned him with glory and honour. (Psalm 8:4-5) But he is to rule out of compassion, not greed. Thus was Adam placed in the Garden of Eden "to work it and take care of it" And the LORD God took the man, and put him into the garden of Eden to dress it and to keep it. (Genesis 2:15).

Another question involves the significance of the terms image and likeness. Most likely these are simply interchangeable terms, as seen by a comparison of Genesis 1:27; So God created man in his *own* image, in the image of God created he him; male and female created he them. Genesis 1:27 with Genesis 5:1;. This *is* the book of the generations of Adam. In the day that God created man, in the likeness of God made he him; Genesis 5:1. They indicate that man is set apart from the rest of creation and is given a position of honor above everything else God has made.

Finally, the fact that the verse concludes with a reference to all the creatures that move along the ground should be noted. This may be designed to lead up to the account of man's fall, which was brought about by the serpent. Adam and Eve should have asserted their dominion over this creature instead of yielding to its seductions. Here man is defined as comprising both male and female. Both share the blessings and responsibilities of being made in the image of God[9].

II. . . . It should seem as if this were the work which he longed to be at; as if he had said, "Having at last settled the preliminaries, let us now apply ourselves to the business, Let us make man." Man was to be a creature different from all that had been hitherto made. Flesh and spirit, heaven and earth, must be put together in him, and he must be allied to both worlds. And therefore God himself not only undertakes to make him, but is pleased so to express himself as if he called a council to consider of the making of him:

Let us make man. The three persons of the Trinity, Father, Son, and Holy Ghost, consult about it and concur in it, because man, when he was made, was to be dedicated and devoted to Father, Son and Holy Ghost. Into that great name we are, with good reason, baptized, for to that great name we owe our being. Let him rule man who said, Let us make man[10].

It has been asserted that as God, (*Eloheem*[3]), is a triune Godhead, that man, in God's image, is also a triune creation. This however is not substantiated by scripture. The Godhead, (*Eloheem*[3]), is that of three separate personages, God the Father, God the Son and God the Holy Ghost; see figure 1. Man however, is only a single entity consisting of three elements, body soul and spirit; see figure 2.

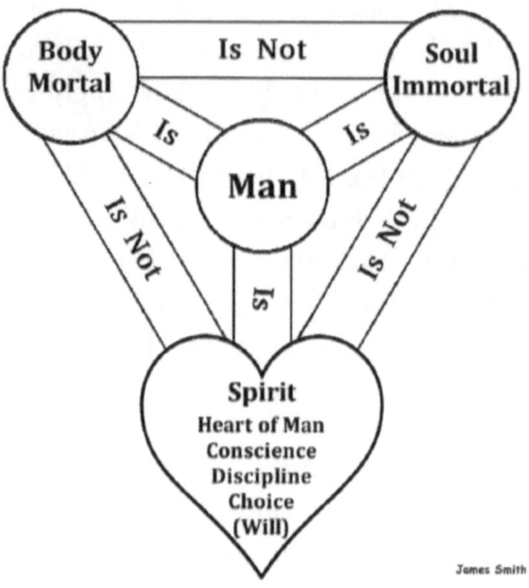

Figure 2 The Nature of Triune Man

The elemental creation of man can best be described like unto a chemical composition. For example glucose, which is a single chemical compound known as blood sugar. It is a compound comprised of three elements, Carbon "C," Hydrogen "H" and Oxygen "O" formulated as $C_6H_{12}O_6$. That is six parts Carbon, combined with twelve parts Hydrogen, and six parts Oxygen, formulating the composition of one molecule of glucose. There are many other compounds made up of these same three chemical elements but in different proportions such a sucrose $C_{12}H_{22}O_{11}$, formaldehyde CH_2O, and acetone C_3H_6O.

Man in the image of God

Man being formed in the image, (*tselem*[8]), of (*Eloheem* [3]) is that he is as a semblance that is a shadow or representative of (*Eloheem*[3]). Man in the image of God; what does this mean in practical terms? It cannot refer to bodily, biological form since God is a Spirit and man is earthly. But while it may be true that the body does not belong to the image, since God does not have a body, yet somehow we would like to see man's body (which is a very real part of man) included in the image. Language and creativity,—two important parts of the image, are impossible without a body. And God the Almighty agreed to share with man dominion and authority over the animal kingdom (Genesis 1:28), an activity in which the whole man, body as well as mind, is involved. Furthermore the Son of God honored the human body by becoming flesh and dwelling among men (John 1:14) (Hebrews 2:14). Lewis suggests that before the Fall, the first man, Adam mirrored Christ the man of Galilee even more nearly than Christ would have resembled his own half-brothers. If this is so, it seems almost blasphemy to consider Adam sired by a shambling ape.

God's attributes shared with man

The main impact of the image is that God endues man with some of his divine attributes, thereby separating and making him different from the beasts. What are these special Godlike qualities which man is permitted to share? I shall mention six: language, creativity, love, holiness, immortality and freedom. You will probably be able to add to this list. All can be summed up by saying that man, like God, has an intelligence, a mind.

Man: The image of God by John Rendle Short March 1, 1981 Originally published in Creation 4, no 1 (March 1981): 21-29.[11]

https://answersingenesis.org/who-is-god/creator-god/man-the-image-of-god © 2018 Answers in Genesis: used by permission /

III. That man was made in God's image and after his likeness, two words to express the same thing and making each other the more expressive; *image* and *likeness* denote the likest image, the nearest resemblance of any of the visible creatures. Man was not made in the likeness of any creature that went before him, but in the likeness of his Creator; yet still between God and man there is an infinite distance. Christ only is the *express* image of God's person, as the Son of his Father, having the same nature. It is only some of God's honour that is put upon man, who is God's image only as the shadow in the glass, or the king's impress upon the coin. God's image upon man consists in these three things: -

1. In his nature and constitution, not those of his body (for God has not a body), but those of his soul. This honour indeed God has put upon the body of man, that the Word was made flesh, the

Son of God was clothed with a body like ours and will shortly clothe ours with a glory like that of his. And this we may safely say, That he by whom God made the worlds, not only the great world, but man the little world, formed the human body, at the first, according to the platform he designed for himself in the fulness of time. But it is the soul, the great soul, of man, that does especially bear God's image. The soul is a spirit, an intelligent immortal spirit, an influencing active spirit, herein resembling God, the Father of Spirits, and the soul of the world.

2. In his place and authority: *Let us make man in our image, and let him have dominion.* As he has the government of the inferior creatures, he is, as it were, God's representative, or viceroy, upon earth; they are not capable of fearing and serving God, therefore God has appointed them to fear and serve man. Yet his government of himself by the freedom of his will has in it more of God's image than his government of the creatures.

3. In his purity and rectitude. God's image upon man consists in knowledge, righteousness, and true holiness, Eph_4:24; Col_3:10. He was upright, Ecc_7:29. He had an habitual conformity of all his natural powers to the whole will of God. His understanding saw

divine things clearly and truly, and there were no errors nor mistakes in his knowledge. His will complied readily and universally with the will of God, without reluctancy or resistance. His affections were all regular, and he had no inordinate appetites or passions. His thoughts were easily brought and fixed to the best subjects, and there was no vanity nor ungovernableness in them.[10]

Man was created a single entity being comprised of three elements, body, (*nephesh*[12]) soul, (*nephesh*[12]), and spirit *(ruach*[6]). The first element of man is the body. The body, (*nephesh*[12]), is the carnal element of man giving physical form and substance to his being, and is the express image of the soul, (*nephesh*[12]).

The second element of man is his soul. The soul, (*nephesh*[12]), is immortal thus it is eternal. Being eternal the soul is in similarity to but not the likeness of God in which man was created. The likeness of God in man being the breath God breathed into Adam to make man a living soul. And the LORD God formed man *of* the dust of the ground, and breathed into his nostrils the breath of life; and man became a living soul. Genesis 2:7. Though the soul of man is immortal, and both the Old and New Testaments speak of the immortality of the soul, the term or designation "immortal soul" in itself is not a biblical doctrine, yet it is a biblical fact.

The third element of man is spirit. The spirit, (*ruach*[6]), is that governing element of man, that when the soul, (*nephesh*[12]), is subpoenaed for judgment, the spirit, (*ruach*[6]), will be that element that will give an accounting of the earthly politics of the soul, (*nephesh*[12]). Then shall the dust return to the earth as it was: and the spirit shall return unto God who gave it. Ecclesiastes 12:7. The spirit, (*ruach*[6]), is the governing element of man's earthly politics.

The first element of man the body, is composed of the dust of this earth and is dependant upon the ecosystem created by (*Eleheem*[3])in Genesis 1:1-26. The order for which the various elements of creation that were made are essential for the intended purpose of sustaining the of life and well being of man. Without the ecosystem in place all creation would soon die due to a deficiency and an imbalance of essential elements required for even the survival of the ecosystem itself.

The second element of man is the soul, (*nephesh*[12]). The soul, (*nephesh*[12]), formed by the breath of God, is the eternal element of the body enabling man to have fellowship with God, (*Eloheem*[3]). The soul, (*nephesh*[12]), can and will only be separated from the body at death. The body which was formed from the dust of the ground will die because of sin, and will be reunited back with the dust of the ground from which it was formed. The soul, (*nephesh*[12]), however, issues from the very breath of God that was breathed into man by (*Eloheem*[3]). The breath of God in the body forms the image of God in which man was created. The soul is immortal and being immortal it is eternal and once created, it will never cease to exist. See figure 2. While the body, (*nephesh*[12]), is mortal, the soul, (*nephesh*[12]) is immortal. I am the God of Abraham, and the God of Isaac, and the God of Jacob? God is not the God of the dead, but of the living. Matthew 22:32.

Man was made last of all the creatures: this was both an honour and a favour to him. Yet man was made the same day that the beasts were; his body was made of the same earth with theirs; and while he is in the body, he inhabits the same earth with them. God forbid that by indulging the body, and the desires of it, we should make ourselves like the beasts that perish! Man was to be a creature different from all that had been hitherto made. Flesh and spirit, heaven and earth, must be put together in him. God said, "Let us make man." Man, when he was made, was to glorify the Father, Son, and Holy Ghost. Into that great name we are baptized, for to that great name we owe our being. It is the soul of man that especially bears God's image. Man was made upright, Eccl 7:29. His understanding saw Divine things clearly and truly; there were no errors or mistakes in his knowledge; his will consented at once, and in all things, to the will of God. His affections were all regular, and he had no bad appetites or passions. His thoughts were easily brought and fixed to the best subjects. Thus holy, thus happy, were our first parents in having the image of God upon them. But how is this image of God upon man defaced! May the Lord renew it upon our souls by his grace[13].

The third element of man is the spirit, (*ruach6*) of man. The spirit is the central governing element of man that forms the *"war room,"* heart, where man's decisions are formulated and finalized, and from where the mandates of those decisions are issued to the body, (*nephesh[12]*), for implementation. There are two main Hebrew words for heart, (*lebab[14]*), which is the interior organ of the body that is responsible for the circulation of blood throughout the body, and (*leb[15]*), which is the command center, *war room*, overseeing the government of the body, (*nephesh[12]*). This command center is the repository for the issues of life. Those life issues, be they good or ignoble, forms the administrating authority that governs the discipline of the soul, (*nephesh[12]*). It is from this command center of the heart, (*leb[15]*), that God through the conscience attempts to instruct and to guide the soul, (*nephesh[12]*), into holiness and righteousness, which is the nature of God, for the intent that the soul, (*nephesh[12]*), would avoid separation from God, once breath is removed from the body, (*nephesh[12]*), with separation from God being the ultimate penalty for sin.

Unlike the animal kingdom that relies on ingrained natural instinct for the governing of their behavior and for the sustenance of their existence, man was created for communion and fellowship with God. For this intended purpose, man as with all other living entities of inelegance, including angels, is given an administrating government of choice for the development of his character. Choice, being the resultant decision that is made after the evaluation of all conflicting arguments and or persuasions arising between two or more opposing factions. Choice is the principal mandate of the heart, *(leb*[15]*)*, which forms the character of the soul. This is not free moral agency.

Choice is not the same as free moral agency. Choice is scriptural, while free moral agency is not. Free moral agency has the connotation that man has the ability to become a god. The Bible actually teaches against free moral agency: God said, for the imagination of man's heart *is* evil from his youth: Genesis 8:21. *It is* not in man that walketh to direct his steps: Jeremiah 10:23b. The heart *is* deceitful above all *things,* and desperately wicked: who can know it? Jeremiah 17:9. yea, also the heart of the sons of men is full of evil,: Ecclesiastes 9:3. the whole world lieth in wickedness. : 1 John 5:19. For we know that the law is spiritual: but I am carnal, sold under sin. 15 For that which I do I allow not: for what I would, that do I not; but what I hate, that do I. 16 If then I do that which I would not, I consent unto the law that *it is* good. 17 Now then it is no more I that do it, but sin that dwelleth in me. 18 For I know that in me (that is, in my flesh,) dwelleth no good thing: for to will is present with me; but *how* to perform that which is good I find not. 19 For the good that I would I do not: but the evil which I would not, that I do. 20 Now if I do that I would not, it is no more I that do

it, but sin that dwelleth in me. 21 I find then a law, that, when I would do good, evil is present with me. Romans 7:14-19. No man can come to me, except the Father which hath sent me draw him: and I will raise him up at the last day. John 6:44. "The phrase 'Free moral agency' is not a scriptural one, any more than the 'immortal soul' is scriptural. Free moral agency is simply a theological expression, man-manufactured for his own convenience, and it may be that it does not express the truth. Let us by all means fit our theology to the Bible, and not try, as many do, to conform the Bible to our theology". (A. P. Adams 1845-1925) For a comprehensive argument of free moral agency and free will vs choice, see the argument of "Free Will" by Arthur P. Adams on line at:
http://www.studyshelf.com/art_adams_freewill.pdf

J. Peston Eby defines free moral agency as: "1. An AGENT is an actor, one who is able to act or perform. 2. A FREE agent is one who can act as he pleases without any restraint of any kind placed upon him. 3. A free MORAL agent is one who is free to act as he pleases and without any restraint on all moral issues, i. e. all questions involving the qualities of right and wrong."

In contrast scripture admonishes us to: Abstain from all appearance of evil. 1 Thessalonians 5:22. The appearance of evil being defined as: Dearly beloved, I beseech *you* as strangers and pilgrims, abstain from fleshly lusts, which war against the soul; 1Peter 2:11. Choice is not just a New Testament doctrine, as a large portion of the Old Testament is God's warning and admonishment to turn away from fleshly lusts that turns the heart and soul from God, as well as His discipline when they refused. Choice was the theme of Joshua's farewell admonition, when he addressed Israel the last time, as his departure from this world loomed before him: And if it seem evil unto you to serve the LORD, choose you this day whom ye will serve; whether the gods which your fathers served that *were* on the other side of the flood, or the gods of the Amorites, in whose land ye dwell: but as for me and my house, we will serve the LORD. Joshua 24:15

The element of choice is the central governing factor controlling the discipline of the heart, (*leb*[15]). The value of the ordinances that issues from the heart, (*leb*[15]) is directly proportional to the outcome of either the benevolence, that is the virtuous persuasion, or the venom, that being the abject persuasion, of all opposing warring factions grappling in the heart, (*leb*[15]). The outcome of those conflicts then becomes the rationale responsible for the governing of the heart, (*leb*[15]): Out of the same mouth proceedeth blessing and cursing. My brethren, these things ought not so to be. 11 Doth a fountain send forth at the same place sweet *water* and bitter? 12 Can the fig tree, my brethren, bear olive berries? either a vine, figs? so *can* no fountain both yield salt water and fresh. James 3:10-12. For this reason Solomon gives solemn warning to maintain diligent vigilance as to what is allowed to be fed into the heart, (*leb*[15]), which is under continuous and constant onslaught by the merciless marauding armies of Satan: Keep (*natsar*[16]) thy heart with all diligence (*mishma*[17]); for out of it *are* the issues of life. Proverbs 4:23.

The Apostle Paul outlines the pharmacology needed to keep (*natsar*[16]) the wellspring of the heart, (*leb*[15]), so that all issues that disseminate from it will be palatable and not nauseous. That pharmacology being, But the fruit of the Spirit is love, joy, peace, longsuffering, gentleness, goodness, faith, 23 Meekness, temperance: against such there is no law. 24 And they that are Christ's have crucified the flesh with the affections and lusts. Galatians 5:22-24. Without this formulary, our heart, (*leb*[15]) will only produce "grapes of thorns" and "figs of thistles" which will only lead to retribution for choosing to neglect the disciplined maintenance required for due spiritual diligence, *mishma*[17] : Now the works of the flesh are manifest, which are *these;* Adultery, fornication, uncleanness, lasciviousness, 20 Idolatry, witchcraft, hatred, variance, emulations, wrath, strife, seditions, heresies, 21 Envyings, murders, drunkenness, revellings, and such like: of the which I tell you before, as I have also told *you* in time past, that they which do such things shall not inherit the kingdom of God. Galatians 5:19-21. Doth a fountain send forth at the same place sweet *water* and bitter? 12 Can the fig tree, my brethren, bear olive berries? either a vine, figs? so *can* no fountain both yield salt water and fresh. James 3:11-12.

As an aid to help discipline his life's choices, man was given a conscience within the heart, (leb[15]) (see figure 2) to supervise the reasoning of his intellect as well as to influence, regulate and maintain orderliness by which to sustain a straight course on the path way of life. The conscience is the inner awareness of the heart, (leb[15]) to a sense of right or wrong that governs the morality of the soul, *nephesh*[12], either to obedience of righteousness: Now the end of the commandment is charity out of a pure heart, and *of* a good conscience, and *of* faith unfeigned: 1 Timothy 1:5, or the rejection of righteousness: Let us draw near with a true heart in full assurance of faith, having our hearts sprinkled from an evil conscience, and our bodies washed with pure water. Hebrews 10:22

It is the decision of each individual if they are going to be obey to the voice of the conscience in obedient submission to holiness which God commands man to be: Speak unto all the congregation of the children of Israel, and say unto them, Ye shall be holy: for I the LORD your God *am* holy. Leviticus 19:2; or hardened by the deceit of depravity for failure to heed the admonition of the conscience: Thus saith the LORD of hosts, the God of Israel; Behold, I will bring upon this city and upon all her towns all the evil that I have pronounced against it, because they have hardened their necks, that they might not hear my words. Jeremiah 19:15.

The repercussions of what the conscience chooses to allow to reside in the heart, leb[15], will determine not only the course of life the soul, *nephesh*[12], will pursue, but also the purpose of life as well: 13 Enter ye in at the strait gate: for wide *is* the gate, and broad *is* the way, that leadeth to destruction, and many there be which go in thereat: 14 Because strait *is* the gate, and narrow *is* the way, which leadeth unto life, and few there be that find it. 15 Beware of false prophets, which come to you in sheep's clothing, but inwardly they are ravening wolves. 16 Ye shall know them by their fruits. Do men gather grapes of thorns, or figs of thistles? 17 Even so every good tree bringeth forth good fruit; but a corrupt tree bringeth forth evil fruit. 18 A good tree cannot bring forth evil fruit, neither *can* a corrupt tree bring forth good fruit. 19 Every tree that bringeth not forth good fruit is hewn down, and cast into the fire. 29 Wherefore by their fruits ye shall know them. Matthew 7:13-20. For every tree is known by his own fruit. For of thorns men do not gather figs, nor of a bramble bush gather they grapes. Luke 6:44.

The conscience: That faculty of the mind, or inborn sense of right and wrong, by which we judge of the moral character of human conduct. It is common to all men. Like all our other faculties, it has been perverted by the Fall (John 16:2; Acts 26:9; Romans 2:15). It is spoken of as "defiled" (Titus 1:15), and "seared" (1 Timothy 4:2). A "conscience void of offence" is to be sought and cultivated (Acts 24:16; Romans 9:1; 2 Corinthians 1:12; 1 Timothy 1:5, 19; 1 Peter 3:21).[18]

Conscience: A persons inner awareness of conforming to the will of God or departing from it, resulting in either a sense of approval or condemnation.

Some people argue erroneously that conscience takes the place of the external law in the Old Testament. However, the conscience is not the ultimate standard of morale goodmess (1Cor. 4:4). The conscience must be formed by the will of God. The law given to Israel was inscribed on the hearts of believers (Heb. 8:10; 10:16); so the sensitized conscience is able to discern God's judgment against sin (Rom. 2:14-15).

The conscience of the believer has been cleansed by the work of Jesus Christ; it nolonger accuses and condems (Heb. 9:14; 10:22). To act contrary to the urging of one's conscience is wrong, for actions that go against the conscience cannot arisre out of faith (1Cor. 8:7-13; 10:23-30)[19].

Thus was the first man Adam was made a living soul

And God said, Let us make man; not Adam alone, but in him the whole human kind, that every man by natural affinity might be taught to love his brother, having all one Father, even God. He gave him a natural but humble name—Adam, or earth, teaching all men to know that they are but worms of the dust[20].

The statement by Joseph Sutcliffe does not set forth nor establish the doctrine of "The universal fatherhood of God and the universal brotherhood of man" which is a doctrine of free masonry, but is simply stating that God as creator has set forth the complexity and diversity of the human race through the original creation of Adam, through whom the complexity of the entire human race would develop and pass on to succeeding generations. For an understanding of the triune makeup of man see figure 2. The Fatherhood of God and the Brotherhood of Man are foundational teachings of Freemasonry.

THE QUESTION OF SIN

Why did God create sin is often asked after a horrific tragedy or event has occurred, or after a catastrophic devastating force of nature, or even after a simple misfortune has happened in a person's life. A clear understanding of the origin of sin can be found by examining scripture.

The prophet Ezekiel gives an insight to the origin of sin: Son of man, take up a lamentation upon the king of Tyrus, and say unto him, Thus saith the Lord GOD; Thou sealest up the sum, full of wisdom, and perfect in beauty. 13 Thou hast been in Eden the garden of God; every precious stone *was* thy covering, the sardius, topaz, and the diamond, the beryl, the onyx, and the jasper, the sapphire, the emerald, and the carbuncle, and gold: the workmanship of thy tabrets and of thy pipes was prepared in thee in the day that thou wast created. 14 Thou *art* the anointed cherub that covereth; and I have set thee *so:* thou wast upon the holy mountain of God; thou hast walked up and down in the midst of the stones of fire. 15 Thou *wast* perfect in thy ways from the day that thou wast created, till iniquity was found in thee. 16 By the multitude of thy merchandise they have filled the midst of thee with violence, and thou hast sinned: therefore I will cast thee as profane out of the mountain of God: and I will destroy thee, O covering cherub, from the midst of the stones of fire. 17 Thine heart was lifted up because of thy beauty, thou hast corrupted thy wisdom by reason of thy brightness: I will cast thee to the ground, I will lay thee before kings, that they may behold thee. 18 Thou hast defiled thy sanctuaries by the multitude of thine iniquities, by the iniquity of thy traffick; therefore will I bring forth a fire from the midst of thee, it shall devour thee, and I will bring thee to ashes upon the earth in the sight of all them that behold thee. 19 All they that know thee among the people shall be astonished at thee: thou shalt be a terror, and never *shalt* thou *be* any more. Ezekiel 28:13-19. In this account, Ezekiel is not referring to the king of Tyre, who Morgan G. Campbell identifies the king as Ithobal, who was a mortal human, but it was against Lucifer who held persuasion over the governing influence of the king of Tyre's heart, leb[15].

This discourse against the king of Tyre is attributed by some as the judgment God pronounced on Jeconiah: *As* I live, saith the LORD, though Coniah the son of

Jehoiakim king of Judah were the signet upon my right hand, yet would I pluck thee thence; 25 And I will give thee into the hand of them that seek thy life, and into the hand *of them* whose face thou fearest, even into the hand of Nebuchadrezzar king of Babylon, and into the hand of the Chaldeans. 26 And I will cast thee out, and thy mother that bare thee, into another country, where ye were not born; and there shall ye die. ... 30 Thus saith the LORD, Write ye this man childless, a man that shall not prosper in his days: for no man of his seed shall prosper, sitting upon the throne of

David, and ruling any more in Judah. Jeremiah 22:24-26, 30. Still others hold it to be judgment on Vatican city and the Catholic church. These views ignore the fact that Ezekiel is referring to a diabolical seraph, equating him to a mortal man. These are not judgments pronounced directly upon man, or against structures or institutions of human design and construction but against Lucifer who is the compelling influence of evil behind all villainous acts who, because of his ignoble action was to become Satan.

Robert Hawker states: From this passage I should be inclined to think that Tyrus is a figure of human nature in general, rather than referring to any one nation in particular; for of what one kingdom upon earth can it be said, that they were perfect in their ways from the day of creation, but of our nature generally speaking. To make application of it to any nation would be to contradict scripture. Those who would refer it to

Papal Rome should seriously consider, that never, at any one period, could such things be said of her. To say, that she hath thrown down her altars, and defiled her sanctuaries, would be to give her what she never had - altars and sanctuaries. Christ is the only New Testament altar, and the true sanctuary of his people[21].

Henry Allen "Harry" Ironside gives a deeper view of this discourse: In verses 11 to 19 the supernatural ruler of Tyre comes before us; though in the latter part of this section we may find it difficult to distinguish between the human and the supernatural, because the one was so completely dominated by the other that his doom was but a picture of that awaiting Satan himself.

It is very evident that of no earthly ruler could these words be spoken. Undoubtedly we have here the original condition and the fall of Satan himself. It was of him that God could say, "Thou sealest up the sum, full of wisdom, and perfect in beauty." Men often ask why God created the devil. The answer is He never created the devil; He created a pure spirit-being of great wisdom and glory, but this spirit dared to conspire against the throne of God, and so the greatest of all the angels became the arch-enemy of God and man.

The prophet says of this spirit leader, "Thou wast in Eden, the garden of God." This would seem to suggest that before man himself was created, this glorious being had charge of the lower creation. There is a mystery here that we may not be able to solve, but Jesus Himself says, "I beheld Satan as lightning fall from heaven" (Luk_10:18). He may have been the one appointed from the beginning to take charge of this world. We do not speak dogmatically, however, as to this, but these verses seem at least to suggest it. Every precious stone was his covering. These precious stones speak of the glories in which God's saints are yet to stand before Him, as we find in the book of Revelation; and here we see them all combined in the robes of this great angelic leader. It was his to lead the praises of the angelic host. The workmanship of his tabrets and of his pipes suggests this: in the day that he was created he was prepared to lead the heavenly choir. He is described as the "anointed cherub that covereth": that is, he was the angel that attended on the throne of God. It was Jehovah Himself who had set him there. He dwelt in the very presence of Deity, walking up and down in the midst of the stones of fire, for we read, "Our God is a consuming fire" (Heb_13:29). He was created perfect, but how long this condition continued we are not told. The Word simply says, "Thou wast perfect in thy ways from the day that thou wast created, till unrighteousness was found in thee."

Verse 16 links the supernatural ruler very closely with the prince who sat on the throne; but God goes on to speak directly of the covering cherub in the following verse, and gives us the secret of his fall. He says, "Thy heart was lifted up because of thy beauty; thou hast corrupted thy wisdom by reason of thy brightness."

The Lord Jesus shows us that Satan is an apostate; he "abode not in the truth" (Joh 8:44). The Apostle Paul instructs Timothy not to put undue responsibility upon a novice, or one newly come to the faith, lest he be lifted up with pride and fall into the condemnation of the devil (1Ti_3:6). This passage is the key to both these other scriptures. It was pride that turned an archangel into a devil.

The closing verses, as we have mentioned, link this great being so intimately with the literal Tyrian ruler that one can hardly be distinguished from the other. Because of the way in which he dominated the heart of the last prince of Tyre, the judgments depicted were to fall[22].

The Bible does give us the best commentary as to whom the prophet Ezekiel was addressing in Ezekiel 28:13-19. The prophet Isaiah states: How art thou fallen from heaven, O Lucifer, son of the morning! *how* art thou cut down to the ground, which didst weaken the nations! 13 For thou hast said in thine heart (*lebab* [14]), I will ascend into heaven, I will exalt my throne above the stars of God: I will sit also upon the mount of the congregation, in the sides of the north: 14 I will ascend above the heights of the clouds; I will be like the most High. Isaiah 14:12-14. It needs to be noted that angels are empyreal beings, of which Lucifer himself is, as such do not have any form of circulatory or respiratory systems in their constitution necessitating an atmosphere as well as nutrients to sustain the maintenance of their being as is the necessity of mortal man. It does not appear that angels, being incorporeal in nature, have a conscience to oversee the governing the discipline of their decisions, yet they apparently have an internal governing authority of choice. For "thou hast said in thine heart" Isiah 14:13, is indicative of choice that has been allocated to empyreal beings who were created for divine service as well as ministering to the sustenance of the saints: Are they not all ministering spirits, sent forth to minister for them who shall be heirs of salvation? Hebrews 1:14. Nothing is known at what time in universal history of eternity past that the angelic host was created. Any argument as to when they were created is only speculation. The only reference we have concerning the angelic origination is the brief description in Ezekiel 28:13-14 of Lucifer, the most elite being of the heavenly host. Lucifer was the anointed, (*mimshach*[23]), cherub and was the epitome of the angelic realm. Harry Ironside said of Lucifer that; "he was the angel that attended on the throne of God."[21]

Apparently becoming disgruntled with the high rank for which he had been created, and either forgetting or ignoring the fact that he was created, Lucifer decided to go head to toe with God, the very one who created him, to be the one who was to eternally rule as the ultimate universal authority. This being the sublimity of brilliant exaulted stupidity. Surely your turning of things upside down shall be esteemed as the potter's clay: for shall the work say of him that made it, He made me not? or shall the thing framed say of him that framed it, He had no understanding? Isaiah 29:16. There isn't any means of calculating the expanse of time in eternity past, so it is not clear how long Lucifer was the protector of God's throne, nor how long the idea of becoming God's superior festered within him, or where that decision even came from, before deciding to implement that ignobly brilliant decision of attempting to usurp ultimate divine authority over God.

Lucifer initiated his demise through a conflict of his egotistical manifesto when he said, "I will ascend into heaven," "I will exalt my throne...," "I will sit...," "I will ascend above...," "I will be like the most high" Isaiah 14:13-14. God however, being thrust into the fray through the arrogance of Lucifer, responded with His divine declaration, "I will cast thee as profane...," "I will destroy thee...," I will cast thee to the ground," "I will lay thee before kings," "I will bring forth a fire...," "I will bring thee to ashes." Ezekiel 28:16-18. The aftermath of this confrontation not only cost Lucifer the stewardship of God's throne, but also banishment from the heavenly courts as well.

In the first account of the germ, or root of sin, occurred in Ezekiel 28:15. Thou *wast* perfect in thy ways from the day that thou wast created, till iniquity (*avel*[24]) was found in thee. The profit Isaiah answers the question of not only what that iniquity was, but also where it emanated from. For thou hast said in thine heart (*lebab*[14]), I will ascend into heaven, I will exalt my throne above the stars of God: I will sit also upon the mount of the congregation, in the sides of the north. Isaiah 14:13. The "iniquity" was Lucifer's decision to stretch his authority beyond the bounds of the limits set by God, to that of being above God, that is superior to God, and above His throne as well. The place where this action originated was from within the governing core of Lucifer's heart (*lebab* [14]). With the constitution of the celestial angelic host being empyreal and not corporeal, and with angels having no need of a circulatory system requiring the need of a heart, for the sustenance of life, yet they do have an inbred self-governing disposition. Lucifer's heart being referred to as (*lebab*[14]), instead of (*leb*[15]), means it is apparent that angels do possibly have a central core of self-administration within their being by which the course of their actions are governed. Angels are obedient to the commands of God, yet they are not empyreal robots as they still have the freedom of choice. Lucifer's heart, (*lebab*[14]), spoken of by Isaiah refers to that inbred self-governing disposition of lucifer's intellect, what ever that may be, which he allowed to influence the decision that initiated his felonious action.

On the authority of scripture, sin had its initial beginnings from conceited loftiness that originated in the governing core of Lucifer's intelligence, that is his heart, (*lebab*[14]). It is only speculation to confirm the cause or source from which pride ignited to influence the arrogance of Lucifer's thinking of, "why should I just only be the guardian of God's throne? As great and powerful as I am, I should be the occupant of that throne." From wherever or whatever the source was, this villainous reasoning festered within the governing core of Lucifer's heart, (*lebab*[14]), until it detonated into egomaniacal pride. As this pride festered from within Lucifer's heart, (*lebab* [14]), possibly from the result of opposing rationales, Lucifer formulated a stratagem to execute his nefarious plan into a course of action. While that scenario was just a thought it was only iniquity, (*avel* [24]), which is the seed from which sin germinates. This being the reason Ezekiel stated Thou *wast* perfect in thy ways from the day that thou wast created, till iniquity (*avel* [24]) was found in thee. Ezekiel 28:15 That seed of iniquity exploded into sin after that thought had been translated into action. It was after the judgment of God upon Lucifer for this action, and after he along with the other angels, under his persuasion who followed him, were expelled from heaven, that Lucifer then became Satan.

Sin does not affect just that individual who has been overpowered by the influence from the seeds of iniquity which they have sown, sin always spreads its effects to others who in some way are associated with that person, or who are in submission to the power, authority, or the governing influence of the perpetrator. One's sin will also negatively impact the affairs of the righteous: And ye, in any wise keep *yourselves* from the accursed thing, lest ye make *yourselves* accursed, when ye take of the accursed thing, and make the camp of Israel a curse, and trouble it.: 1 But the children of Israel committed a trespass in the accursed thing: for Achan, the son of Carmi, the son of Zabdi, the son of Zerah, of the tribe of Judah, took of the accursed thing: and the anger of the LORD was kindled against the children of Israel.:

20 And Achan answered Joshua, and said, Indeed I have sinned against the LORD God of Israel, and thus and thus have I done: Joshua 6:18; 7:1 & 20. The sin of one man brought God's wrath upon the nation Israel, just as Adam's sin brought death upon the entire human race. Wherefore, as by one man sin entered into the world, and death by sin; and so death passed upon all men, for that all have sinned: Romans 5:12.

There are also scriptural references referring to other angels of the celestial host that also fell with Lucifer when he was cast out of heaven. Much discussion has been made concerning these fallen angels and demons. The discussion between fallen angels and demons, and the number of angels under Lucifer's influence that fell with him, is a subject for another argument. The subject of this argument is sin, its origin, its cause, its administration as well as freedom from. This is why God gave us the admonishment through the wisdom of king Solomon: 1 My son, forget not my law; but let thine heart keep my commandments: 2 For length of days, and long life, and peace, shall they add to thee. 3 Let not mercy and truth forsake thee: bind them about thy neck; write them upon the table of thine heart: 4 So shalt thou find favour and good understanding in the sight of God and man. Proverbs 3:1-4. The writer of Hebrews reiterates Solomon's admonition: 1 Therefore we ought to give the more earnest heed to the things which we have heard, lest at any time we should let *them* slip. 2 For if the word spoken by angels was stedfast, and every transgression and disobedience received a just recompence of reward; 3 How shall we escape, if we neglect so great salvation; which at the first began to be spoken by the Lord, and was confirmed unto us by them that heard *him;* Hebrews 2:1-3. Jesus Himself gives us clear and final warning: 3 Remember therefore how thou hast received and heard, and hold fast, and repent. If therefore thou shalt not watch, I will come on thee as a thief, and thou shalt not know what hour I will come upon thee. Revelation 3:3. The heart referred to in Proverbs 3:1 & 3 is (*leb*[15]) the repository of the conscience. The reasoning for this admonition is that when the soul is subpoenaed to account of the deeds done in the body, the constitution of the heart, (*leb*[15]), at that time will become either an eternal legally binding asset: For with the heart man believeth unto righteousness; and with the mouth confession is made unto salvation. Romans 10:10; or liability: For out of the heart proceed evil thoughts, murders, adulteries, fornications, thefts, false witness, blasphemies: Matthew 15:19.The heart referred to in Romans 10:10 and Matthew 15:19 is (*kardia*[25]), the same inference as the Hebrew word (*leb*[15]), referring to the heart, (*leb*[15]), as the central governing nucleus of man's character, that is the conscience, from within the spirit the third element of the man. See fig. 2.

As long as iniquity, which is the seed of the sin, remains confined to the (*karida*[24]), it is a benign intention of the soul (*nephesh*[12]). That intention becomes malignant sin when it has been acted upon by the body, (*nephesh*[12]), Though iniquity in the heart, leb[15] may be benign, yet the psalmist David declared: If I regard iniquity (*aven*[26]), in my heart (*leb*[15]), the Lord will not hear *me:* Psalm 66:18. As iniquity, (*aven*[26]), is the seed of sin, it must be removed from the heart (*leb*[15]), before it becomes a malignant nefarious exploit that will result in spiritual death, (*epithanatios*[27]), which will ultimately lead to eternal separation from God if not repented of, for not having been removed from the heart (*karida*[24]), while it was yet benign, not having become a malignant action. The benign seeds of iniquity allowed to reside in the heart, (*leb*[15]), will always geminate into a malignant action of sin outside of the heart, (*leb*[15]). Review Ezekiel 28:13-19 as well as Isaiah 14:13-14 for a reminder of what will happen if iniquity, (*aven*[26]), is not removed from the heart (*leb*[15]).

Though Lucifer was banished from heaven, he was still empyreal and still retained most if not all of the attributes with which he was created. Being ousted from heaven, Lucifer still had at least limited access to part of the heavenly realm: Now there was a day when the sons of God came to present themselves before the LORD, and Satan came also among them. 7 And the LORD said unto Satan, Whence comest thou? Then Satan answered the LORD, and said, From going to and fro in the earth, and from walking up and down in it. Job 1:6-7. This scene is repeated in Job 2:1-2. With a holy God allowing the epitome of evil into the courts of heaven, especially into His presence is the subject of another argument. The reference to "the sons of God" in Job 1:6 and 2:1 is itself a debatable issue, yet for this current argument, it will be assumed they are angels, which view is held by a few commentators.

The Pulpit Commentary: Now there was a day when the sons of God came to present themselves before the Lord. By "the sons of God" it is generally admitted that, in this place, the angels are meant (so again in Job_38:7). The meaning of the phrase is probably different in Gen_6:2. Angels and men are alike "sons of God," as created by him, in his image, to obey and serve him. Christ, the "Only Begotten," is his Son in quite a different sense.[29]

Joseph Benson Commentary: Now there was a day — A certain time appointed by God; when the sons of God came — The Targum says, Troops of angels, the LXX., Angels of God; the holy angels are called sons of God, (Job_38:7, and Dan_3:25; Dan_3:28,) because of their creation by God, their resemblance of him in power, dignity, and holiness, and their filial affection and obedience to him. To present themselves before the Lord[30]

John Gill's Exposition: This is generally understood of the angels, as in Job 38:7 who may be thought to be so called, because of their creation by the father of spirits, and their likeness to God in holiness, knowledge, and wisdom, and being affectionate and obedient to him; as also on account of the grace of election, and confirmation in Christ bestowed upon them.[31]

John Wesley's Notes: A day - A certain time appointed by God. The sons - The holy angels, so called, chap. xxxviii, 7 Da 3:25,28, because of their creation by God, for their resemblance of him in power, and dignity, and holiness, and for their filial affection and obedience, to him. Before - Before his throne, to receive his commands, and to give him an account of their negotiations.[32]

The question arises as to why God, (*Eloheem*[3]), chose earth to be man's habitat knowing that it was Satan's realm. Being disenfranchised of his former angelic position, Satan became as it were a wandering star establishing his domain wherever in the nether regions of God's created universe. That wherever may or may not have been earth before the creation of man. The Bible, God's revelation of warnings, which are given for instruction, as well as for the eternal salvation of man, only gives us limited insight concerning Satan and his activities. The bible is not an comprehensive source of information giving an unequivocal accounting of his person. Yet the Bible often correlates people such as the king of Tyre Ezekiel 28:13, as well as places and events with satanic inference.

The Bible is not for presenting a character study of Satan, but rather a warning to us to not only be on guard against his attacks that will come on every saint of God, especially those who are lax in their spiritual vigilance, but also insight to his means and modus operandi: Be sober, be vigilant; because your adversary the devil, as a roaring lion, walketh about, seeking whom he may devour: 9 Whom resist stedfast in the faith, knowing that the same afflictions are accomplished in your brethren that are in the world. 1 Peter 5:8-9. The Apostle states that Satan is as the likeness of a roaring lion, while only becoming a roaring lion ripping apart and shredding the soul when vigilance is neglected. The Bible also instructs us that the best way to be vigilant against satanic onslaughts is to: Put on the whole armour of God, that ye may be able to stand against the wiles of the devil. 13 For we wrestle not against flesh and blood, but against principalities, against powers, against the rulers of the darkness of this world, against spiritual wickedness in high *places*. Ephesians 6:11-12. The Bible explicitly warns us as to why we should always be vigilant and girded with spiritual armor: 14 And no marvel; for Satan himself is transformed into an angel of light. 15 Therefore *it is* no great thing if his ministers also be transformed as the ministers of righteousness; whose end shall be according to their works. 2 Corinthians 11:14-15 Failure to comply with admonished Biblical instructions, leaves the soul, nephesh[12], subject to satanic persuasion. Lest Satan should get an advantage of us: for we are not ignorant of his devices. 2 Corinthians 2:11.

However, since God chose earth to establish man whom He created for fellowship, along with the environment necessary for man's existence, that Satan, vehemently obsessed with passion to be worshiped as the supreme god, chose the nether regions of earth, if he had not already done so, to organize and establish his domain from which to launch his attack upon man, God's ultimate creation in his retaliation against God. Satan, being God's adversary, and impassioned with the obsession of being worshiped as the supreme god, seeks to profane all that he can of God's creation in his striving to usurp divine authority away from God.

When God created Adam, sin under the dominion of Satan, the author of sin, was already in full force and effect in the world: For until the law sin was in the world: but sin is not imputed when there is no law. Romans 5:13. For this cause, after placing man in the garden paradise that had been created for him, and God knowing it was Satan's haunt, as well as knowing his wiles, gave man a stern warning, "law," to be obeyed without question: And the LORD God took the man, and put him into the garden of Eden to dress it and to keep it. 16 And the LORD God commanded the man, saying, Of every tree of the garden thou mayest freely eat: 17 But of the tree of the knowledge of good and evil, thou shalt not eat of it: for in the day that thou eatest thereof thou shalt surely die. Genesis 2:15-17. God always gives a warning before He strikes with the desire that He would not have to strike at all. So to protect the man from the potential onslaught that eventually over powered him, God gave Adam one commandment that was to be obeyed. Adam's choice emerged from the conflict between obedience to God's commandment, or the submission to the deception of satanic persuasion that was evidenced before him, of no harm coming upon Eve after she first ate of the forbidden fruit. After weighing the conflicting arguments between God's law, And the LORD God commanded the man, saying, Of every tree of the garden thou mayest freely eat: 17 But of the tree of the knowledge of good and evil, thou shalt not eat of it: for in the day that thou eatest thereof thou shalt surely die (*muth*[33]). Genesis 2:16-17. and satanic deception: Now the serpent was more subtil than any beast of the field which the LORD God had made. And he said unto the woman, Yea, hath God said, Ye shall not eat of every tree of the garden? 2 And the woman said unto the serpent, We may eat of the fruit of the trees of the garden: 3 But of the fruit of the tree which *is* in the midst of the garden, God hath said, Ye shall not eat of it, neither shall ye touch it, lest ye die. 4 And the serpent said unto the woman, Ye shall not surely die: 5 For God doth know that in the day ye eat thereof, then your eyes shall be opened, and ye shall be as gods, knowing good and evil. Genesis 3:1-5, Adam chose to believe the satanic deception that had been amplified by an agreeable argument from Eve who had previously partaken of the fruit without any adverse consequences to her physical appearance. And when the woman saw that the tree *was* good for food, and that it *was* pleasant to the eyes, and a tree to be desired to make *one* wise, she took of the fruit thereof, and did eat, and gave also unto her husband with her; and he did eat. Genesis 3:6.

So you say that Genesis 3:1-5 is dealing with Eve, and not Adam. Even though Eve misquoted God's command, she was still aware of God's command to

Adam concerning abstaining from eating of the fruit. Instead of invoking God's authority given to Adam, to have dominion over the earth Genesis 1:26, to which she was also an authorized agent of, she chose to relinquish her God given authority over the deception of Satan. However, the intent of this argument is not to debate the actions of either Adam or Eve as there has been much published and preached concerning that issue. The point in question is to show that there is always conflict, sometimes acutely severe conflict, between opposing conflicting arguments from which a person's heart, (*leb*[15]), must chose to obey. At issue here is that after Eve made the choice to eat of the fruit, she then persuaded Adam to eat as well. Adam had to decide if he was going to be obedient to either God's command, or to the persuasion of the visibly deceptive evidence of there not being any apparent change in Eve's physical disposition as she was still alive, after having been victimized by Satan's deception. Adam was just as guilty as Eve since knowing what God had commanded him as well as the consequence for disobedience. Adam chose to partake of Eve's deception in the transgression, instead of being obedient to God's command. Adam did not have to do it, he chose to violate God's commandment making him just as guilty as Eve.

Adam choosing the route of disobedience by partaking of the forbidden uit resulted in the eyes of them both being opened which revealed their nakedness: And the eyes of them both were opened, and they knew that they *were* naked: and they sewed fig leaves together, and made themselves aprons. Genesis 3:7. Before their disobedience Adam and Eve were apparently clothed with either a shekinah light from God or some other form of divine glory, (*kabod*[34]). What ever the covering was, it was the essence of purity and holiness and therefore incapable of being stained by sin. It was therefore removed from Adam and Eve as a result of Adam's disobedience.

Most people have little understanding of what the Shekinah Glory of YEHOVAH God is, let alone realize the prophetic significance of this manifestation of God. The Jewish rabbis coined this extra-biblical expression, and it is form of a Hebrew word that literally means "he caused to dwell" -- signifying that it was a divine visitation of the presence or dwelling of YEHOVAH God on this earth. In order to fully understand the prophetic passages in the book of Revelation, we need to thoroughly grasp the concept of the physical manifestations of our Creator God.

This is very important. The word "Shekinah" (Sh'khinah) was coined from verbal cognates (related words) in the Bible which describe the "presence" of YEHOVAH God in a certain locality. The verbal cognates are used extensively to describe the "Shekinah" appearances. The word "Shekinah" itself is not found in the Biblical texts, but the concept clearly is. The word most certainly is derived from "shakan," and whoever first used the word "Shekinah" coined it as a substantive (noun form) from the verbal forms used to describe the "abiding, dwelling, or habitation" of the physical manifestations of YEHOVAH God described in Exodus 24:16, 40:35 and Numbers 9:17-18 -- and various other places where "shakan" is used.

In the Encyclopedia Judaica the "Shekinah" is defined as "the Divine Presence, the numinous immanence of God in the world,...a revelation of the holy in the midst of the profane...." (Volume 14, pp. 1349-1351).

"One of the more prominent images associated with the Shekhinah is that of light. Thus on the verse, '... the earth did shine with His glory' (Ezekiel 43:2), the rabbis remark, 'This is the face of the Shekhinah' (Avot diRabbi Natan [18b-19a]; see also Chullin 59b-60a). Both the angels in heaven and the righteous in olam ha-ba ('the world to come') are SUSTAINED BY THE RADIANCE OF THE SHEKINAH (Exodus Rabbah 32:4, B'rakhot 17a; cf. Exodus 34:29-35)....

"According to Saadiah Gaon [882-942 C.E.], the Shekhinah is identical with kevod ha-Shem (the glory of God"), which served as an INTERMEDIARY BETWEEN GOD AND MAN during the prophetic experience. He suggests that the "glory of God" is the Biblical term, and Shekhinah the Talmudic term for the created splendor of light which ACTS AS AN INTERMEDIARY BETWEEN GOD AND MAN, and which sometimes TAKES ON HUMAN FORM. Thus when Moses asked to see the glory of God, HE WAS SHOWN THE SHEKHINAH, and when the prophets

in their visions saw God in HUMAN LIKENESS, what they actually saw WAS NOT GOD HIMSELF BUT THE SHEKHINAH (see Saadiah's interpretation of Ezekiel 1:26, I Kings 22:19, and Daniel 7:9 in Book of Beliefs and Opinions 2:10)."
http://hope-of-israel.org.nz/glory.htm   Used   by permission, Hope of Israel Ministries

Shekinah [shuh KIGH nuh] *(dwelling)*
A visible manifestation of the presence of God (also spelled Scechinah and Shekhinah). Although the word is not found in the Bible, it occurs frequently in later Jewish writings. It refers to the instances when God showed himself visibly, as for example, on Mount Sinai, (Ex. 24:9-18) and in the Most High Place of the tabernacle, and in Solomon's temple. The Shekinah was a luminous cloud that rested above the altar in the place of worship and lit up the room. when the Babylonians destroyed the temple, the shekinah glory vanished. There was no shekinah in the temple rebuilt later under Zerubbabel and Herod.[35]

Regardless the form with which they were covered, God, being a holy God disapproves of unrestricted flagrant nudity, especially in His presence. Adam and Eve apparently understood this as conviction of the still small voice of the conscience rose in their heart, *leb*[15], prompting them to cover themselves after they saw that they were naked, which they attempted to do with fig leaves. The demand for the covering of the body is further evidenced by the instructions God gave Moses for the design as well as the requirements for the wearing of the garments by the high priest, as well as the subordinate priests. These garments were required to be worn when they came into the presence of God within the tabernacle to minister the duties of the priest's office. And for

Aaron's sons thou shalt make coats, and thou shalt make for them girdles, and bonnets shalt thou make for them, for glory and for beauty. 41 And thou shalt put them upon Aaron thy brother, and his sons with him; and shalt anoint them, and consecrate them, and sanctify them, that they may minister unto me in the priest's office. 42 And thou shalt make them linen breeches to cover their nakedness; from the loins even unto the thighs they shall reach: 43 And they shall be upon Aaron, and upon his sons, when they come in unto the tabernacle of the congregation, or when they come near unto the altar to minister in the holy *place*; that they bear not iniquity, and die: *it shall be* a statute for ever unto him and his seed after him. Exodus 28:40-43. For a further study see Principles of Purity by Bill Burkett on line at:
http://actsion.com/?s=principles+of+purity.

After partaking of the forbidden fruit, whatever they were clothed with was removed revealing their nakedness. It was at this point that they both experienced spiritual death *epithanatios*[27] which was not physical death, but spiritual death which caused the eternal separation of all mankind from the presence of God. As the result of Adam's sin, the entire lineage of man became contaminated by sin. Wherefore, as by one man sin entered into the world, and death by sin; and so death passed upon all men, for that all have sinned: Romans 5:12. This contamination of sin is passed genetically as well as inherently to all of Adam's progeny. This is the death knell to the process of man being returned back to the ground from which he was taken, and that being the reward of Adam's sin. Eve having been formed from a rib of Adam, as well as being a partaker with Adam in the transgression, was to follow him in physical death as well.

The question now arises as to what sin really is

Sin is not a creation. Sin not a noun, it is a verb as it always has been and always will be an action, stemming from choice. Sin is the willful violation of divine jurisprudence as well as the willful refusal or neglect to act in accordance to divine jurisprudence.

SIN - Lawlessness (1John 3:4) or transgression of God's will, either by omitting to do what God's law requires or by doing what it forbids.

Mankind was created without sin, morally upright and inclined to do good (Eccl. 7:29). But sin entered into human experience when Adam and Eve violated the direct command of God by eating the forbidden fruit in the Garden of Eden (Gen. 3:6). Because Adam was the head and representative of the whole human race, his sin affected all future generations (Rom. 5:12-21). Associated with this guilt is a corrupted nature passed from Adam to all his descendants. Out of this perverted nature arise all the sins that people commit (Matt. 15:19); no person is free from involvement in sin (Rom. 3:23) [36].

The origin of sin was Lucifer's attempt to become god. Sin is the legacy left to us, after the consummation of that first heinous action of Adam. Sin is always an action that emanates from seeds of iniquity, (*aven*[26]), that are allowed to reside in the heart, (*leb*[15]). The instigator of sin being Lucifer, who having allowed a seed of iniquity to fester within him until it became his overlord, driving his nefarious actions to extend his God given authority to that of himself being superior to God as well as God's authority. In short he became his own god, the ultimate goal and ambition of freewill and free morale agency. Sin is the consequence of ignoble choice and or decision. Sin is a violation of God's law.

Law was even before all creation. Law is the foundation upon which the entire universe is structured as well as upon witch it functions. Without law all of creation, even if it could exist, would be nothing but a huge massive pile of debris. Without law, even that pile of debris would not be able to exist for there would not be a foundation for its existence: Then the LORD answered Job out of the whirlwind, and said, 4 Where wast thou when I laid the foundations of the earth? declare, if thou hast understanding. 5 Who hath laid the measures thereof, if thou knowest? or who hath stretched the line upon it? 6 Whereupon are the foundations thereof fastened? or who laid the corner stone thereof; 8 Or *who* shut up the sea with doors, when it brake forth, *as if* it had issued out of the womb? 9 When I made the cloud the garment thereof, and thick darkness a swaddlingband for it, 10 And brake up for it my decreed *place*, and set bars and doors, 11 And said, Hitherto shalt thou come, but no further: and here shall thy proud waves be stayed? 19 Where *is* the way *where* light dwelleth? and *as for* darkness, where *is* the place thereof, 20 That thou shouldest take it to the bound thereof, and that thou shouldest know the paths *to* the house thereof? 22 Hast thou entered into the treasures of the snow? or hast thou seen the treasures of the hail, 23 Which I have reserved against the time of trouble, against the day of battle and war? 24 By what way is the light parted, *which* scattereth the east wind upon the earth? 25 Who hath divided a watercourse for the overflowing of waters, or a way for the lightning of thunder; 26 To cause it to rain on the earth, *where* no man *is; on* the wilderness, wherein *there is* no man; 27 To satisfy the desolate and waste *ground;* and to cause the bud of the tender herb to spring forth? Job 38:1, 4-6, 8-11, 19-20, 22-27. It is the authority of divine law that enables order to be established throughout the universe.

The Cassini-Huygens Mission, which ended in 2017, was, by any stretch of the imagination, a remarkable human achievement. Launched on October 15, 1997, the craft was active for nearly 20 years before its final descent into the oblivion of Saturn's gravity on September 15, 2017. The use of the Internet in schools was in its infancy, but I remember, as a teacher, using the school's IT laboratory with students to track the launch and to find information on how it was going to get to Saturn.

Cassini-Huygens took seven years to reach Saturn. In order to save fuel, an extremely complicated orbit was calculated to use planetary gravitational fields to accelerate the craft enough for its long journey to Saturn. This involved two close approaches to Venus, one to the Earth, and another to Jupiter, which finally whipped the craft off in the right direction for the rendezvous with the ringed planet and its moons.

The complexity of the calculations required to power the craft to Saturn relied on the predictability and measurability of gravitational forces elsewhere in the Solar System. Such confidence in calculations was only possible because these universal constants display the wisdom of God. NASA's brilliant scientists did not assume that their work would be hindered by random evolutionary chance in the way that all these planets behaved. Yet, part of their mission was the vain search for the evolution of life on one of Saturn's moons. Evolution-minded scientists often cannot see the irony or the inconsistency of such an approach – a reliance on divine design in an attempt to prove such design does not exist[38]!

With God's word being the natural law ruling and controlling the existence and order of all creation, it is also the ultimate irrefutable authority establishing the code of conduct by which man's life is to be governed. As with the natural law of motion discovered by Sir Isaac Newton, whose third law of motion states, "for every action there is an equal and opposite reaction," so too with divine jurisprudence, for every act or action of disobedience, there is an equal and opposite, act, reaction and or consequence.

The negative action or consequence of violating divine jurisprudence may not always be immediate as it is with the natural physical laws of motion, yet it will happen. The results of violating divine jurisprudence may not come to fruition until after death, (*epithanatios*[27]). When Adam therefore partook of the forbidden fruit, he willingly of his own volition (action) removed himself from being under God's authority (reaction) which placed him under the authority of satanic mastery (consequence) as the result of his action. The consequence of Adam's action resulted in spiritual death (*epithanatios*[27]), that is death of the soul, (*nephesh*[12]) resulting in man being eternally separated from God. The terminating effect (consequence) of spiritual death, (*epithanatios*[27]), is physical death, (*thanatos*[28]). All go unto one place; all are of the dust, and all turn to dust again. Ecclesiastes 3:20, At which time all souls, (*nephesh*[12]), will acknowledge the truth of all creation. 11 For it is written, *As* I live, saith the Lord (*Kurios*[5]), every knee shall bow to me, and every tongue shall confess to God. 12 So then every one of us shall give account of himself to God. Romans 14:11-12.

At this time of judgment all violations of divine jurisprudence will be accounted for: And as it is appointed unto men once to die, but after this the judgment: 28 So Christ was once offered to bear the sins of many; and unto them that look for him shall he appear the second time without sin unto salvation. Hebrews 9:27-28. Spiritual death, (*epithanatios*[27]), is the result of satanic lust to be worshiped as god. The sole ambition of sin is for the perpetrator of sin to be worshiped as god. This is the sole purpose of the legacy that has been passed on to all succeeding generations of Adam, that is for man to become a god, owing their allegiance to Satan: For as by one man's disobedience many were made sinners, so by the obedience of one shall many be made righteous. Romans 5:19. We cannot avoid physical death, but we can live above the effects that satanic mastery has placed upon the soul, *nephesh*[12], causing the soul to be eternally separated from God, (*epithanatios*[2]): Prove all things; hold fast that which is good. 22 Abstain from all appearance of evil. 1 Thessalonians 5:21-22. The verdict between life and death, (*epithanatios*[26]), of every individual is issued by the decree given from the governing authority that is allowed to reside in the heart, (*leb*[15]), be it righteous or ignoble: For if ye live after the flesh, ye shall die: but if ye through the Spirit do mortify the deeds of the body, ye shall live. Romans 8:13.

With angels being empyreal, whatever the authority is within their constitution that governs their decision making procedure, is unknown. Yet apparently factions emanated from within Lucifer caused him to be confronted with the compelling proposition to exalt his position above God. This action was apparently spawned by the seed of pride, which brought about his condemnation. It may have been self induced pride alone that caused Lucifer to respond as he did. Whatever and or wherever these negative characteristics emanated from is only speculation. They were however, of contemptible inducement which was not of God. As Lucifer yielded to the persuasion of iniquity, the cause of his attempt to exalt himself above God, man in like manner allows the persuasion of iniquity to further separate himself from God, as iniquity is always the seed of sin. And have no fellowship with the unfruitful works of darkness, but rather reprove *them*. Ephesians 5:11.

SIN AFFECTS THE ENVIRONMENT

Unlike Satan who is a spirit entity, and is without restricted confinement to a physical local for his habitation, man being mortal, is restricted to the confines of this earth from which he was created, for the limits of his habitation. Both Satan and man have been separated from the presence of God by a single act of sin. Satan through pride and Adam through satanic deception. Adam's sin not only bequeathed a sin nature to all his posterity that will be engendered through him, of whom we are a part of: For we know that the law is spiritual: but I am carnal, sold under sin. Romans 7:14, but his sin also bequeathed a curse on the environment in which man needs to exist. And unto Adam he said, Because thou hast hearkened unto the voice of thy wife, and hast eaten of the tree, of which I commanded thee, saying, Thou shalt not eat of it: cursed *is* the ground for thy sake; in sorrow shalt thou eat *of* it all the days of thy life; 18 Thorns also and thistles shall it bring forth to thee; and thou shalt eat the herb of the field; 19 In the sweat of thy face shalt thou eat bread, till thou return unto the ground; for out of it wast thou taken: for dust thou *art*, and unto dust shalt thou return. Genesis 3:17-19

This legacy Adam bequeathed to us began its endowment with the rise of the vile immoral carnal nature of man: And GOD saw that the wickedness of man *was* great in the earth, and *that* every imagination of the thoughts of his heart *was* only evil continually. 6 And it repented the LORD that he had made man on the earth, and it grieved him at his heart. 7 And the LORD said, I will destroy man whom I have created from the face of the earth; both man, and beast, and the creeping thing, and the fowls of the air; for it repenteth me that I have made them. Genesis 6:5-7 Even though God repented of His creation of man, He still found that a seed of righteousness was still evident in the heart, *leb*[15], of man: But Noah found grace in the eyes of the LORD. These *are* the generations of Noah: 9 Noah was a just man *and* perfect in his generations, *and* Noah walked with God. Genesis 6:8-9:

"In the six hundredth year of Noah's life, in the second month, the seventeenth day of the month, the same day were all the fountains of the great deep broken up, and the windows of heaven were opened. And the rain was upon the earth forty days and forty nights."

The Flood began with two geophysical events – the bursting forth of Fountains of the Great Deep and the opening of the Windows of Heaven. But what could these events have actually looked like?

Starting with the Fountains of the Great Deep, this would appear to be a reference to volcanic activity. We can envisage cracks opening up in deep points of the pre-Flood ocean. Possibly magma came through these cracks, but also we expect that a lot of super-heated water would emerge, thrown at supersonic speed high into the atmosphere. In other words, these fountains would have been similar to the ocean floor springs that exist today, but on a larger and more violent scale. This would have been the main source of the overwhelming majority of the floodwaters which covered the Earth. And after the water had been thrown high into the

atmosphere, it would have returned to the Earth as torrential rain, so this is probably what is meant by the Windows of Heaven – more correctly, the Floodgates of Heaven. There would not have been enough moisture in the pre-Flood atmosphere to produce the amount of flood water required, whereas the mechanism suggested, called Catastrophic Plate Tectonics, flows from Scripture, and seems to fit scientific observations. Notes: Ref: Snelling, A. (2009),
Earth's Catastrophic Past, Master Books, pp. 275-276.
https://creationmoments.com/sermons/fountains-of-the-deep-3/

Even though Noah found grace in the sight of God, yet being a descendant of Adam, Noah was still an heir to Adam's legacy that has been passed to all humanity, which he could not deny or refuse. Though the flood caused the annihilation of all that drew breath, it had non effect on the legacy bequeathed to humanity by Adam, as sin is the end result of iniquity that issues from the command center of man's heart, (*leb*[15]). Noah, like it or not was still an heir to Adam, and being an heir, he was still under the same judgment as Adam: For *there is* not a just man upon earth, that doeth good, and sinneth not. Ecclesiastes 7:20.

With the survival of Noah, the legacy left to us by Adam is still in full force and effect. Yet with the foul aroma of the odious stench of death hanging over all the earth, resulting from the sentence of the flood judgment, a sweet bouquet soon filled the atmosphere as Noah offered a sacrifice to God: And Noah builded an altar unto the LORD; and took of every clean beast, and of every clean fowl, and offered burnt offerings on the altar. 21 And the LORD smelled a sweet savour; and the LORD said in his heart, I will not again curse the ground any more for man's sake; for the imagination of man's heart *is* evil from his youth; neither will I again smite any more every thing living, as I have done. While the earth remaineth, seedtime and harvest, and cold and heat, and summer and winter, and day and night shall not cease. Genesis 8:20-22 This decree is not a license for contemptible licentiousness as: The eyes of the LORD *are* upon the righteous, and his ears *are open* unto their cry. 16 The face of the LORD *is* against them that do evil, to cut off the remembrance of them from the earth. Psalm 34:15-16. Divine jurisprudence has not been affected by the adjudication of the flood.

The argument now centers on the cursed earth of Genesis 3:17 and the apparent removal of that curse as is implicated in Genesis 8:21.

And unto Adam he said, Because thou hast hearkened unto the voice of thy wife, and hast eaten of the tree, of which I commanded thee, saying, Thou shalt not eat of it: cursed *is* the ground for thy sake; in sorrow shalt thou eat *of* it all the days of thy life; Genesis 3:17. Cursed in Genesis 3:17 is the Hebrew word 'arar: - Strong's number H779, defined as A primitive root; to *execrate:* - X bitterly curse. The reason for this curse is the ultimate result of Adam's transgression as is explained by the Hebrew word sake, awboor, Strong's number H5668 meaning: Passive participle of H5674; properly *crossed*, that is, (abstractly) *transit*; used only adverbially on *account* of, in *order* that: - because of, for (. . . 's sake), (intent) that, to. It was because of Adam's sin that the earth was cursed. The prime reason being that the ground is the very element from which Adam was created. In short, man brought the curse upon himself as well as upon the very element from which he was created, all because of his disobedience to God's law. Strong's Hebrew and Greek Dictionaries e-Sword bible software Execrate means: to revile, despise, detest, loathe, hate, decry, abhor, denounce, condemn, to damn. Arar simply means that Adam's choice to disobey God is the cause for the earth being cursed, so that it would no longer bring forth an abundant harvest as it did before the transgression. Arar is also the same word God used when He pronounced judgment upon the serpent for his deception of Eve, Genesis 3:14.

The curse referenced in Genesis 8:21 that God said He would not again invoke upon the ground is the Hebrew word qalal - kaw-lal' Strong's number H7043, defined as: A primitive root; to *be* (causatively *make*) *light*, literally (*swift, small, sharp*, etc.) or figuratively (*easy, trifling, vile*, etc.): - abate, make bright, bring into contempt, (ac-) curse, despise, (be) ease (-y, -ier), (be a, make, make somewhat, move, seem a, set) light (-en, -er, ly, -ly afflict, -ly esteem, thing), X slight [-ly], be swift (-er), (be, be more, make, re-) vile, whet. Strong's Hebrew and Greek Dictionaries: e-Sword Bible software Qalal used in Genesis 8:21 did not remove the curse 'arar' that was pronounced on the ground in Genesis 3:17, it just mitigated the ultimate effect the original curse had on the ground. God simply alleviated the original judgment of the curse arar to the lesser charge of qalal in Genesis 8:21. The ground will always remain under the curse, qalal for the duration of the descended linage of Adam as long as earth shall endure. The decree "neither will I again smite any more every thing living, as I have done" simply states that future floods would be local or regional, and not global. The ground will still produce a diet of thorns and thistles as: cursed *is* the ground for thy sake; in sorrow (*itstsabon*[37]) shalt thou eat *of* it all the days of thy life; Thorns also and thistles shall it bring forth to thee; and thou shalt eat the herb of the field; Genesis 3:17b -18. The flooding has been alleviated, but the sorrow, *itstsabon*[37], i.e. agony required to produce a harvest for the sustenance of life has not.

"Although the imagination of man's heart should be evil, i.e. should they become afterwards as evil as they have been before, I will not destroy the earth by a Flood."[38]

And the Lord said in his heart. *Ie.* resolved within himself. It is not certain that this determination on the part of Jehovah was at this time communicated to the patriarch (*cf., Gen_6:3, Gen_6:7*) for Divine inward resolves which were not at the moment made known unless the correct reading be *to his (Noahs) heart,* meaning the Lord *comforted* him *(cf. Jud_1:19:3; Rth_2:13; Isa_40:2; Hos_2:14)* which is barely probable. I will not again curse the ground any more for man"s sake. Literally, *I will not add to curse.* Not a revocation of the curse of Gen_3:17, nor a pledge that such curse would not be duplicated. The language refers solely to the visitation of the Deluge, and promises not that God may not some. times visit particular localities with a flood, but that another such world-wide catastrophe should never overtake the human race. For the imagination of man"s heart is evil from his youth[39]

The curse on the ground however, can and will only be removed in the day the earth is judged by fire: Knowing this first, that there shall come in the last days scoffers, walking after their own lusts, 4 And saying, Where is the promise of his coming? for since the fathers fell asleep, all things continue as *they were* from the beginning of the creation. 5 For this they willingly are ignorant of, that by the word of God the heavens were of old, and the earth standing out of the water and in the water: 6 Whereby the world that then was, being overflowed with water, perished: 7 But the heavens and the earth, which are now, by the same word are kept in store, reserved unto fire against the day of judgment and perdition of ungodly men. 2 Peter 3:3-7 For as the new heavens and the new earth, which I will make, shall remain before me, saith the LORD, so shall your seed and your name remain. 23 And it shall come to pass, *that* from one new moon to another, and from one sabbath to another, shall all flesh come to worship before me, saith the LORD. 24 And they shall go forth, and look upon the carcases of the men that have transgressed against me: for their worm shall not die, neither shall their fire be quenched; and they shall be an abhorring unto all flesh. Isaiah 66:22-24.

Sin can only be extricated by blood!

Questions have risen as to why God allowed sin to continue after iniquity (*avel*[24]) was first revealed in lucifer. God could have immediately confined Lucifer to his eternal punishment, the lake of fire, thus putting to an end to his and only to his Iniquity, (*avel*[24]) as his iniquity was the result of his personal choice. However, had God confined Lucifer to the lake of fire, the issue that caused iniquity to fester within Lucifer would not have been addressed. That issue being the ignoble government of the heart (leb[15]). There isn't any other biblical reference as to the origin of iniquity, and the only thing we know about the origin of iniquity is that it began with Lucifer. The iniquity, (*avel*[24]), found in Lucifer was an exploit initiated by his own individual decision issuing from the government of his heart, (*lebeb*[14]). Any physical action against Lucifer at this time would not have prevented iniquity, *avel*[24], from arising again from somewhere else either within the ranks of the celestial host, nor would it prevent iniquity from eventually rising up from within man whom He intended to create: The heart *is* deceitful above all *things,* and desperately wicked: who can know it? 10 I the LORD search the heart, *I* try the reins, even to give every man according to his ways, *and* according to the fruit of his doings. Jeremiah17:9-10. This deceitfulness is nothing more then man desiring to be god, the same as it was and still is with Satan. Any arguments about iniquity arising from another source had Lucifer been banished to the lake of fire for his reward for his initial act of iniquity, is a defunct issue, as the cause of the original source of iniquity is unknown, yet the product of iniquity is the result of choice, making choice the logical genesis of iniquity.

Had God chosen the path of annihilation to deal with sin, the consequence of iniquity, speculation would possibly spread like wild fire throughout the heavenly realm that God must be terrified of sin. At issue with this is, how can the eternal creator, the absolute supreme authority of the creation of the entire universe and all things therein, be terrified of anything? God would also be criticized for being a domineering tyrant, which in some circles he probably is anyway. In today's society He would be considered an iniquiophobic, that is being intolerant of the rights of iniquity, or as being a right wing bigot, by those opposing themselves against God: Because that, when they knew God, they glorified *him* not as God, neither were thankful; but became vain in their imaginations, and their foolish heart was darkened. Romans 1:21. These comments are nothing but a slap in the face of God. In all probability God knew from the beginning of creation the probability of evil arising from somewhere within the ranks of the heavenly host to challenge His authority. If not from within the heavenly realm, then the probability is that it would arise from within the mortal realm which was His intended plan for creation. God looked down from heaven upon the children of men, to see if there were *any* that did understand, that did seek God. 3 Every one of them is gone back: they are altogether become filthy; *there is* none that doeth good, no, not one. Psalm 53:2-3. For this cause, a simple warning, i.e. law governing the design for man's relationship to God was given to Adam, before he ever encountered Satan, which law was and still is to be a guide for man to enter into a deep relationship with God his creator.

Iniquity, (*avel*[24]), is a compelling force issued from the design of nefarious appetites generated from the government within the spirit of man, the heart, (*leb*[15]). That force will either be upheld and executed by the lusts of the flesh: For all that *is* in the world, the lust of the flesh, and the lust of the eyes, and the pride of life, is not of the Father, but is of the world. 1 John 2:16; or nixed by the discipline of the governing authority of the conscience: And the world passeth away, and the lust thereof: but he that doeth the will of God abideth for ever. 1 John 2:17. Once the seed of iniquity, (*avel*[24]), is ingrained in the heart, (*leb*[15]) and executed by choice, sin is then the controlling element of the body, (*nephesh*[12]).

Rather then dealing with every single case of iniquity, (*avel*[24]), that would arise, from any quarter, a time has been set for earth to be judged of sin: 15:1 And I saw another sign in heaven, great and marvellous, seven angels having the seven last plagues; for in them is filled up the wrath of God. 16:1 And I heard a great voice out of the temple saying to the seven angels, Go your ways, and pour out the vials of the wrath of God upon the earth. Revelation 15:1 & 16:1.

At the set time, the Lord Himself will lead His army of saints into battle against all adherents of iniquity: And Enoch also, the seventh from Adam, prophesied of these, saying,

Behold, the Lord cometh with ten thousands of his saints, 15 To execute judgment upon all, and to convince all that are ungodly among them of all their ungodly deeds which they have ungodly committed, and of all their hard *speeches* which ungodly sinners have spoken against him. Jude 1:14-15.

On that day the course of sin will be left powerless to inflict further casualties and will meet its final judgment. O let the nations be glad and sing for joy: for thou shalt judge the people righteously, and govern the nations upon earth. Selah. Psalm 67:4. An execution date has been set for the total obliteration of sin, as well as judgment upon all God's creation: And I saw a great white throne, and him that sat on it, from whose face the earth and the heaven fled away; and there was found no place for them. 13 And I saw the dead, small and great, stand before God; and the books were opened:

and another book was opened, which is *the book* of life: and the dead were judged out of those things which were written in the books, according to their works. 13 And the sea gave up the dead which were in it; and death and hell delivered up the dead which were in them: and they were judged every man according to their works. 14 And death and hell were cast into the lake of fire. This is the second death. 15 And whosoever was not found written in the book of life was cast into the lake of fire. Revelation 20:11-15.

God has reserved the time of judgment for Himself and has not revealed it to anyone: But of that day and *that* hour knoweth no man, no, not the angels which are in heaven, neither the Son, but the Father. Mark 13:32. God still holds out the invitation for sinful man to repent of his evil ways, but that too will also have an end. At that time the entire universe will be eradicated of all sin and iniquity. The Lord is not slack concerning his promise, as some men count slackness; but is longsuffering to us-ward, not willing that any should perish, but that all should come to repentance. 10 But the day of the Lord will come as a thief in the night; in the which the heavens shall pass away with a great noise, and the elements shall melt with fervent heat, the earth also and the works that are therein shall be burned up. 11 *Seeing* then *that* all these things shall be dissolved, what manner *of persons* ought ye to be in *all* holy conversation and godliness, 2 Peter 3:9-11

God's remedy for the eradication of sin

When God pronounced judgment upon Adam and Eve, He also implemented the antidote for sin where by man could be reconciled back to Himself. This was initiated by the slaying of at least two animals in the making of the coats for Adam and Eve. Unto Adam also and to his wife did the LORD God make coats of skins, and clothed them. Genesis 3:21 The blood of innocent animals that was shed, was a temporal atonement that was to be made for the cleansing of sin, but not the cleansing from sin, which blood pointed to the Lamb of God who was to shed his blood as the ultimate propitiation for sin as well as man's cleansing from sin: For if, when we were enemies, we were reconciled to God by the death of his Son, much more, being reconciled, we shall be saved by his life. 11 And not only *so*, but we also joy in God through our Lord Jesus Christ, by whom we have now received the atonement (*katallage*[41]). Romans 5:10-11. It was the blood and not the animal skins that was the acceptable clothing for Adam and Eve. For the life of the flesh *is* in the blood: and I have given it to you upon the altar to make an atonement for your souls: for it *is* the blood *that* maketh an atonement for the soul. Leviticus 17:11.The making of those coats showed man the futility of his attempt to rectify the wanton indulgement of his disobedience, sin, by means of his carnal methods of attempted damage control. The only damage control for sin is: That if thou shalt confess with thy mouth the Lord Jesus, and shalt believe in thine heart that God hath raised him from the dead, thou shalt be saved. Romans 10:9. That decision must be confessed from conviction within the heart, (*leb*[15]), not just with indulgent verbiage of the mind.

Tragedies, an unwelcome accounting of iniquity

Salvation is the only means through which man can be reconciled back to God. It does not answer any of the questions concerning issues of: Oh! NO! HOW?...... WHY?. Many questions arise out of the myriads of tragedies, catastrophes, afflictions, devastations, adversities, anguish, distress, desolations, upheavals, calamities, and sorrows which befall all mankind, even on the redeemed of God. Many of these disasters stem from the violation of law, even from adverse interaction of opposing reactions between natural forces such as tsunamis, tornados, hurricanes, earthquakes and volcanos.

Mount St. Helens located in Skamania County, in Washington state that erupted on May 18, 1980, was the most violent and powerful volcano in the continental US. It was from the result of a series of earthquakes and steam venting eruptions. Mount St. Helens was a composite volcano of multiple layers of lava and ash, referred to as a stratovolcano. A composite volcano frequently vent through violent explosions.

The build up of magma at a shallow depth below the volcano caused by seismic activity resulted in a large bulge and fracture on the north slope of the mountain. The earthquake also caused a hole in the volcano causing the magma chamber to split allowing magma to rise up to the main vent. The forward movement of magma followed the physical path of least resistance of escape which was sideways through the fracture in the bulge on the north side of the mountain, instead of vertically through the top of the mountain.

It was known that Mount Saint Helens was heading for an eruption, verified by showing signs of activity. Some authorities were convinced that the mountain was heading for an eruption, while some non-authoritarians were not convinced. Having been restless for about two months, speculation of an eruption was a question of when, not if. The sideways explosion as well as the size of the eruption caught all officials off guard. For more information on the eruption of Mount Saint Helens see: http://science.answers.com/Q/What_was_the_causes_of_eruption_of_Mt_St_Helens

Tragedies are also the result of man altering the course of God's original design of earth's landscape by diverting water courses, the building of dams to reclaim land etc. Tragedies also occur when man violates sound reasoning by building houses or even cities in areas where man has altered the scope of earth's original landscape, or even within the flood plane of a natural water course.

Dr. James Morris, director of University of South Carolina's Belle W. Baruch Institute for Marine and Coastal Sciences near Georgetown, South Carolina, notes that the wetlands around the city of New Orleans are disappearing at such ar ate that, by the end of this century, there will be very little left of the marshlands.

"I'm more involved in the technical aspects of how you go about restoring the marshes. One of the solutions is to divert river flow from the Mississippi into the surrounding bayous," Morris said. "That's probably the only feasible solution."

And that's just what the U.S. Army Corps of Engineers have done during the recent flooding of the Mississippi River, as they opened two channels to divert part of the Mississippi River away from New Orleans and through the floodways towards the wetlands.

The Bonnet Carre spillway is sending water into Lake Pontchartrain, while the Morganza spillway diverts water through the Atchafalaya River Basin and into the Gulf of Mexico.

As a result, the starving Delta wetlands are fed with the much needed sediments that they need to grow and thrive, while only a thousand or so humans are affected.

"But the question is, 'Do you flood a city of a million people or do you flood 1,000 homes in a floodway?' The answer to that one is pretty easy. That was designed from the get go. People who lived there knew that was going to happen," Morris said. "Yes, it's a tragedy for some people, but no one died, no one lost their land. They'll rebuild. And the city of New Orleans survived."

So maybe there's a lesson to be learned here: live in balance with nature, instead of trying to make nature live in subservience to you.
http://planetsave.com/2011/06/13/diverting-the-mississippi-to-revive-wetlands/. Used by permission

These altered landscapes are arenas where tragedies are most likely to occur. The devastation of New Orleans by Hurricane Katrina for an example. For a history of the land reclamation of New Orleans see: http://neworleans.danellis.net/land_reclamation.htm.

Disasters can also be caused simply by human neglect, such as building a campfire or igniting fireworks in a dry timber area whose sparks ignite massive forest fires. Disasters have also been caused by the introduction of non-indigenous animal species into a specific locale for the intent of pest control, only to have those species to become hazardous themselves simply by not having a natural enemy in their new environment. For more information on the hazzards of non-indigenous animal species see: http://mentalfloss.com/article/12760/1 1-invasive-species-wreaking-havoc-around-world

Ecological issues have been caused by exotic animals bought as pets that have been released into similar yet unnatural environments by irresponsible pet owners, who were either no longer able, or unwilling to care for them. In the last decade the Everglades National Park has seen a variety of different species of snakes from around the world invading its domain, the Burmese python being the main breed. On August 23, 1922 when hurricane Andrew struck Florida a number of exotic wildlife facilities were devastated, one of which was a breeding facility for Burmese pythons. The devastation of that facility resulted in over 1,000 pythons escaping their enclosures to be released into the wild. Snake owners also, who bought the reptiles as small babies, after finding they were too large or too burdensome to keep also released pythons into the wild. The actual origin of the snakes induction may never be known, however, South Florida, especially the Everglades is now home to thousands of Burmese pythons.

The natural habitat of the python being tropical, semi arid forests, marshes, grasslands, swamps and rainforests, made the Everglades is an ideal climate for them to survive in. They also survive in woodlands and foothills that are in close proximity of where there is a constant reliable source of water which is necessary for their survival, making the Everglades a suitable environment for the non-indigenous reptile. Basically a terrestrial snake, Burmese pythons are fully capable of swimming, and have the ability to remain underwater for a maximum of 30 minutes without having to come up for air.

The reason for the rapid increase in the Florida python population is that a female Burmese python after mating, may lay up to 100 eggs however, the average amount is about 12-36. The eggs are protected by the female until they are hatched, after which she leaves them to fend for themselves. Burmese pythons routinely live for about 25 years, and will grow to 12 feet in length, with some growing to a length of 23 feet. The python can weigh up to 200 pounds and is ranked as the third largest snake in the world.

The Burmese python has become the scourge of the Florida wetlands. These pythons are devastating the everglade ecology by their consumption of native mammals such as raccoons, foxes, opossums, rabbits and other small game as well as much of the bird population. Animals that are not in the python's food chain, such as native snakes being left unable to find rabbits and other small rodents to feed on, suffer as the result of their food supply being consumed by the pythons. A reduction in the Burmese python prey, such as racoons, contributes to an increase in turtle population as fewer racoons are feeding on their eggs. With this ecology imbalance the migration of the python can be expedited as their food chain diminishes with the increase of their population. With the python's population increase and the decrease in their food chain, python's will tend to migrate up the east coast and parts of the west, as these locals provide suitable climates to allow for the python's cross country expansion, only to reek havoc on the ecology of these new habitats as well.

Burmese pythons are also a distinct threat to domestic animals such as pets, small livestock and even humans. A 10-foot long python can easily kill a child and a 15-foot long snake can overpower and kill a human adult. These python's haven even been known to eat deer and alligators.

For more information on pythons being responsible for decimating the Everglades[42]

Other calamities that occur are simply the result of natural disasters, as well as man's violation of natural laws. These are all part of the judgment that was pronounced on Adam as a result of his disobedience to God's command. And unto Adam he said, Because thou hast hearkened unto the voice of thy wife, and hast eaten of the tree, of which I commanded thee, saying, Thou shalt not eat of it: cursed *is* the ground (*adamah*[43], earth) for thy sake; in sorrow shalt thou eat *of* it all the days of thy life; 18 Thorns also and thistles shall it bring forth to thee; and thou shalt eat the herb of the field; 19 In the sweat of thy face shalt thou eat bread, till thou return unto the ground; for out of it wast thou taken: for dust thou *art*, and unto dust shalt thou return. Genesis 3:17-19.

Calamities that befall us are just some of thorns and thistles that have infested the ground of this earth, (*adamah*[43]). Calamities are simply part of the bread diet of thorns and thistles that is given for our consumption as a result of the "sweat of thy face labor." This diet is also part of the bequest that has been passed to us through Adam. The results of man's labor derived from the nourishment of a thorns and thistle diet will eventually culminate with corrosion, erosion, rust, rot, or decay, which conditions themselves ultimately lead to other forms of disaster. For an example of the effects of deteriation see the report on the San Francisco Bay Bridge Bolt Failure on line at: https://www.nace.org/CORROSION-FAILURES-San-Francisc o-Bay-Bridge-Bolt-Failure.aspx

Another of those disasters is the calamities of war, which is simply a continuation of the conflict orchestrated by Cain against his brother Able: And Cain talked with Abel his brother: and it came to pass, when they were in the field, that Cain rose up against Abel his brother, and slew him. Genesis 4:8. A retort by many in an attempt to refute the claim that war is a continuation of this conflict, is that God Himself ordered His people many times to engage in armed conflict with the enemies of Israel. And the LORD spake unto Moses in the plains of Moab by Jordan *near* Jericho, saying, 51 Speak unto the children of Israel, and say unto them, When ye are passed over Jordan into the land of Canaan; 52 Then ye shall drive out all the inhabitants of the land from before you, and destroy all their pictures, and destroy all their molten images, and quite pluck down all their high places: 53 And ye shall dispossess *the inhabitants* of the land, and dwell therein: for I have given you the land to possess it. Numbers 33:50-53. True, yet God uses man's own devices, such as war as a means of controlling and or removing thorns and thistles from the ground, (*adamah*[43]), that are a violation of His eternal plan, or even part of the continuation thereof.

Many would argue that God could revoke His curse upon the ground. The earth, because of man's sin is under the judgment of God because of that sin. The curse brought upon on the earth as the result of Adam's transgression can and will only be revoked or removed when God himself destroys and recreates the universe: But the day of the Lord will come as a thief in the night; in the which the heavens shall pass away with a great noise, and the elements shall melt with fervent heat, the earth also and the works that are therein shall be burned up. 11 *Seeing* then *that* all these things shall be dissolved, what manner *of persons* ought ye to be in *all* holy conversation and godliness, 12 Looking for and hasting unto the coming of the day of God, wherein the heavens being on fire shall be dissolved, and the elements shall melt with fervent heat? 2 Peter 3:10-12. This scheduled renovation was reiterated by the Apostle John the revelator: And I saw a new heaven and a new earth: for the first heaven and the first earth were passed away; and there was no more sea. Revelation 21:1, and even verified by God Himself: And he (God) that sat upon the throne said, Behold, I make all things new. And he said unto me, Write: for these words are true and faithful. Revelation 21:5. This is but a brief summation of understanding the questions, How?... Why? on a global or national scale.

But what about calamities that befall on a personal level? On a personal level many calamities occur simply by being at the wrong place at the wrong time. Some calamities could have been avoided if a person would have paid attention to the inner prompting, that arise within the heart, (*leb*[15]), through the still small voice of the conscience. Often these warnings go unheeded simply because they counter the heart's, (*leb*[15],) desire for the fulfilling the lustful cravings of our carnal appetites, or that they come at a most inopportune time or we just do not want to be bothered at the present time. By ignoring the inner prompting arising from the voice of the conscience, we press on to fulfill the passions that have been dictated to us from the lusts of the heart, (*leb*[15],) which often leads to the detriment of our own well being. I speak from the rubble of my own experiences of many times ignoring the entreaties of my own heart, *leb*[15], which often led to my own hurt. There are times however, that we may simply be innocent victims of the evil designs of others to which there is not always the benefit of a satisfactory explanation.

At times we may be victims of our own bad decisions and or choices, which often leads to some form of damage such as the loss of life, limb, property or any combination of the three. We often hear the news how some individual or individuals visiting other countries, especially those with repressive governments, that have been arrested by those governments because those visitors violated the governing laws of those repressive governments, such as taking something without paying for it, or without receiving authorized permission to have it, simply because they want it for a souvenir. This is nothing but an act of theft that has been executed by the governing administration of the perpetrator's heart, (*leb*[15]) for which there is no justification for their lustful greed. Then people and governments of other nations get upset and outraged at the cruel treatment those perpetrators have received as the result of the harsh punishment administered to them by those repressive regimes. People of democratic governments then begin demanding that their government officials intervene on the behalf of the guilty perpetrators. Yes it is that the penalties for the violation of the law of the offended countries are often extremely severe, and the cruelty of their treatment of the perpetrators is often inhumane especially to foreigners. However, the perpetrators themselves are the victims of their own ignominious actions, and not victims of the tyrannical state. These perpetrator's brought the ruthless treatment of these governments upon themselves. They can not blame anybody or anything else for the sentence imposed upon them by the courts but they themselves. If those perpetrators did not have an appetite for thorns and thistles, and would not have acted upon the influence of the iniquitous appetites of their heart, (*leb*[15]), they would not have engaged in the conduct that caused them to violate the legitimate laws of those dictatorial governments. The outcry should be against the guilty offenders and not against the offended governments! No, this is not a defense of or for coercive governments! It is placing the blame where the blame belongs, that being upon the perpetrator themself. HELLO! **SIN IS A CRUEL TASKMASTER!**

If democratic governments were really concerned about the ill treatment of repressive governments against the offenders of their laws, they would pressure those regimes to amend the harsh penalties demanded by their law for those crimes. They would also pressure those governments for the humane treatment of the offenders, especially against offenders that are visitiors from foreign countries. However, if the government of the heart, (*leb*[15]), of the perpetrator is: Ye shall not steal, neither deal falsely, neither lie one to another; Levicitus 19:11, then the violation of their laws would never have occurred in the first place. For rulers are not a terror to good works, but to the evil. Wilt thou then not be afraid of the power? do that which is good, and thou shalt have praise of the same: 4 For he is the minister of God to thee for good. But if thou do that which is evil, be afraid; for he beareth not the sword in vain: for he is the minister of God, a revenger to *execute* wrath upon him that doeth evil. 5 Wherefore *ye* must needs be subject, not only for wrath, but also for conscience sake. Romans 13:3-5.

Every legal government has the judicial right to formulate their own laws, as well as the penalties for the violation of those laws, without the approval or disapproval of outside governments. However, the penalty for law violation should be based on reasonable canon: But we know that the law *is* good, if a man use it lawfully; 9

Knowing this, that the law is not made for a righteous man, but for the lawless and disobedient, for the ungodly and for sinners, for unholy and profane, for murderers of fathers and murderers of mothers, for manslayers, 10 For whoremongers, for them that defile themselves with mankind, for menstealers, for liars, for perjured persons, and if there be any other thing that is contrary to sound doctrine; 1 Timothy 1:8-10. If the laws of repressive governments were respected, observed and obeyed, there would not be any violations. The issue always lies with the government of the perpetrator's heart, (*leb*[15]) not with the laws of repressive governments. HELLO! ARE YOU LISTENING?

Often times calamities entrap us when we cultivate the seeds of abject iniquities which frequently assail us, simply because we elect to ignore the warning of "Do not eat of the forbidden fruit" that is hanging so appetizingly before us cajoling us to reach out and to partake of it with the intent of enslaving the soul. After we blatantly partake of that fruit, having ignored the warnings coming to us through the still small voice of the conscience emanating from the command center of our heart, (*leb*[15]), we wonder why we wind up enthroned again in a bed of thorns and thistles. Apparently it is because we prefer a hard irritating scratchy bale of weeds to rest our tired weary bodies on, instead of a soft firm torso conforming comfortable mattress of righteousness. The choice dear pilgrim is ours, mine as well as yours! Just don't complain when your bed of weeds catches on fire with you in it and you are unable to escape. You have had ample warning! THIS IS NOT THE CRYING OF WOLF!

We may even find ourselves to be victims of following the bad advice of others, as with Abraham concerning Ishmael: And Sarai said unto Abram, Behold now, the LORD hath restrained me from bearing: I pray thee, go in unto my maid; it may be that I may obtain children by her. And Abram hearkened to the voice of Sarai. Genesis 16:2. We know the results of that decision! Maybe so-called friends have caused you to be a guinea pig that is caught holding the bag of evidence left from the fraudulent actions of others who have violated one or more of either Gods commands, the rule of judicial governmental laws and or both, simply because you desired the wages they agreed to pay. This desire for thorns and thistles will often lead to a duplicitous fraudulent companionship: I wrote unto you in an epistle not to company with fornicators: 10 Yet not altogether with the fornicators of this world, or with the covetous, or extortioners, or with idolaters; for then must ye needs go out of the world. 11 But now I have written unto you not to keep company, if any man that is called a brother be a fornicator, or covetous, or an idolater, or a railer, or a drunkard, or an extortioner; with such an one no not to eat. 1Corinthians 5:9-11. The violation of God's commands or governing judicial law will ultimately lead to an unpleasant diet of thorns and thistles. I know from experience that jail house cuisine is not gourmet dining, especially for those who happen to be coffee connoisseurs.

The relationships we often pursue is another major cause of the calamities that ensnare us. Often times the mystique of a woman, or the mannerism of a suave handsome debonair man attracts our affection. However, when we find that these often unworthy individuals do not aspire to the same high morale or spiritual code of conduct we have dedicated our lives to, we so willfully defend them and continue pursuing the relationship simply because of the false contagious facade their influence is having over us. The tragic outcome of these relationships are varied and numerous which often leave one in despair, even to the point of absolute devastation which often leads to murder and or suicide.

The deterioration of morale values, the spurning of our ethics, all leads to a catastrophic damning effect on the soul, (*nephesh*[12]). Business partnerships, our circle of friends, often brings us to chaotic ruin. Be ye not unequally yoked together with unbelievers: for what fellowship hath righteousness with unrighteousness? and what communion hath light with darkness? 15 And what concord hath Christ with Belial? or what part hath he that believeth with an infidel? 2 Corinthians 6:14-15. But we still continue to engage in their pursuit simply because our bottom line is, we prefer a carnal diet of thorns and thistles over heavenly manna. This being evidenced by the rejection of God's laws and commands: And what agreement hath the temple of God with idols? for ye are the temple of the living God; as God hath said, I will dwell in them, and walk in them; and I will be their God, and they shall be my people. 17 Wherefore come out from among them, and be ye separate, saith the Lord, and touch not the unclean *thing*; and I will receive you, 18 And will be a Father unto you, and ye shall be my sons and daughters, saith the Lord Almighty. 2 Corinthians 6:14-18. The rejection of God's laws is the acceptance of satanic deception. You will be obedient to one or the other, but not to both! Know ye not, that to whom ye yield yourselves servants to obey, his servants ye are to whom ye obey; whether of sin unto death, or of obedience unto righteousness? Romans 6:16.

Many times man perpetrates personal tragedies by the actions he inflects on his own body, (*nephesh*[12]). These actions can be 1. the result of alcoholism: cirrhosis of the liver, high blood pressure and related heart problems, intestinal ulcers and other internal problems. 2. The results of smoking: cancer, respiratory diseases, cardiovascular diseases, various affects on unborn children. 3. The results of drug addiction: mood swings, depression, anxiety, paranoia, violence; complication of mental illness; Hallucinations; confusion; desire to do ever-increasing amounts of the drug; the engaging in risky sensual behavior resulting in contraction of HIV, hepatitis and other STD illnesses; heart rate irregularities, heart attack; respiratory problems such as lung cancer, emphysema and other breathing problems; abdominal pain, vomiting, constipation, diarrhea; Kidney and liver damage; seizures, stroke, brain damage; changes in appetite, body temperature and sleeping patterns. 4. The result of bad dietary issues such as gluttony: nutrient deficiency, obesity, chronic disease, diabetes, hypertension, cancer, osteoporosis, mental disorders. These are but a few of the self induced tragedies that a person can suffer because of self induced ignoble indulgences they have inflected on themselves.

So how is it possible for these actions to inflict calamities on the body, (*nephesh*[12])? Know ye not that ye are the temple of God, and *that* the Spirit of God dwelleth in you? 17 If any man defile (*phtheiro*[44]) the temple of God, him shall God destroy (*phtheiro*[44]); for the temple of God is holy, which *temple* ye are. 1 Corinthians 3:16-17. Many are the preachers who will adamantly proclaim that destroy in 1 Corinthians 3:17 means eternal damnation in the lake of fire. They fail to realize that defile and destroy in 1 Corinthians 3:17 is the same Greek word (*phtheiro*[44]). To paraphrase this verse could be to say: *If any man will willfully defile, phtheiro[44], his body which is the temple of God, God will cause his body to be devastated, or even destroyed, (defiled), (phtheiro[44]) from the debilitating effects of the ignoble actions he has, of his own free choice, inflicted on his own body.* Why would God do this? He doesn't, it is the end result of our own choice as, the temple of God is holy and we are commanded to be holy as well: But as he which hath called you is holy, so be ye holy in all manner of conversation; 16 Because it is written, Be ye holy; for I am holy. 1 Peter 1:15-16.

The body of the spiritual soul is the temple of God the soul of whose heart, (leb), is established by faith, while the body of the carnal soul is the temple of the god of this world, the soul of whose heart, (leb), is the web of Satan, the god of this world. Holiness shows the world who truly dwells in the residence of our bodies, God or the god of this world. Regardless of who we may claim occupies the temple of our body, our actions will always overpower our words exposing the true identity of that occupant, as actions are always speaking so loudly that it cannot be heard what the voice is saying. Since the body of the righteous is the temple of God we need to be obedient not only to the word of God, but also to that voice through which God attempts to communicate with our heart, (*leb*[15]), by the agency of the conscience concerning our demeanor both public and private: And the LORD spake unto Moses, saying, 2 Speak unto all the congregation of the children of Israel, and say unto them, Ye shall be holy: for I the LORD your God *am* holy. Leviticus 19:1-2. To the faithful, obedience to this command carries with it an eternal weight of glory: Follow peace with all *men*, and holiness, without which no man shall see the Lord: Hebrews 12:14. There are also dire warnings for disobedience: For the wrath of God is revealed from heaven against all ungodliness and unrighteousness of men, who hold the truth in unrighteousness; 19 Because that which may be known of God is manifest in them; for God hath shewed *it* unto them. 20 For the invisible things of him from the creation of the world are clearly seen, being understood by the things that are made, *even* his eternal power and

Godhead; so that they are without excuse: 21 Because that, when they knew God, they glorified *him* not as God, neither were thankful; but became vain in their imaginations, and their foolish heart was darkened. Romans 1:18-21. The only way we can see God or even please Him is: Having therefore these promises, dearly beloved, let us cleanse ourselves from all filthiness of the flesh and spirit, perfecting holiness in the fear of God. 2 Corinthians 7:1.

God can but usually does not interfere with the choice man makes from the decisions of the heart, (*leb* [15]). However, at times, God will attempt to guide man's decisions through conviction of the conscience or by the inner prompting of the heart, (*leb* [15]), of booth the spiritual soul as well as the carnal soul. God can and will also intervene at times when in the face of unavoidable disaster. Several times during those years spent in rebellion on the back side of Calvary when I lived a carnal lifestyle, God has dealt with my conscience, and even intervened on my behalf a few times when I was in physical danger. Once one morning as I was driving to work, as I approached a line of cars stopped for a red traffic light, my attempt to stop only revealed the fact that the breaks on my car had no intention of engaging, rendering me helpless. Out of where ever, I felt as if a hand had become a restraining barrier in front of my car bringing me to a complete stop preventing me from crashing into the back of the car ahead of me. I could not see it, yet I actually felt the force that, that hand exerted on my car bringing me to a safe stop.

God has instilled in the conscience of every soul, (*psuche*[40]), the carnal as well as the spiritual, a sense of right and wrong. Our decision is the determining factor as to which course we will allow our soul to pursue. That being honorable unto righteousness, or contemptible unto putrefaction. God will also intervene in the intended election of human affairs when human devices interfere with His divine eternal plan. However, human devices have the potential of being returned upon the perpetrator's own head: The heathen are sunk down in the pit *that* they made: in the net which they hid is their own foot taken. 16 The LORD is known *by* the judgment *which* he executeth: the wicked is snared in the work of his own hands. Psalm 9:15-16. So they hanged Haman on the gallows that he had prepared for Mordecai. Then was the king's wrath pacified. Esther 7:10, for: Whoso diggeth a pit shall fall therein: and he that rolleth a stone, it will return upon him. Proverbs 26:27.

As long as this earth, (*adamah*[43]), stands there will always be thorns and thistles, as they are the byproduct of sin. The question is; How do you prefer your diet of thorns and thistles: raw, fried, baked, broiled, sauteed, on the half shell, bar-b-que, in a casserole, as a smoothie, or a toping for ice cream how? A la mode? A la carte? You can not escape thorns and thistles, you can not rid them of yourself, but there is weed control: A sower went out to sow his seed: and as he sowed, some fell by the way side; and it was trodden down, and the fowls of the air devoured it. 6 And some fell upon a rock; and as soon as it was sprung up, it withered away, because it lacked moisture. 7 And some fell among thorns; and the thorns sprang up with it, and choked it. 8 And other fell on good ground, and sprang up, and bare fruit an hundredfold. And when he had said these things, he cried, He that hath ears to hear, let him hear. Luke 8:5-8. The decisions that arise victoriously out of the melee between the lusts of the flesh and the restraint of the conscience will be the governing factor that will validate the condition of the ground of the heart, (*leb*[15]), exposing it to be rocky, thorny, or good, ground. The weed infestation of the heart's, (*leb*[15]), ground is determined by the governing authority of our choices. The deciding factor that will determine the type of ground the heart, (*leb*[15]), will be, is influenced by wether the body is the temple of God or the web of Satan. Nothing has to be done for Satan to have dominion over the web of your heart, (*leb*[15]), for he already has that control by the authority of Adam's transgression, and by our being an heir of Adam's legacy. For I know that in me (that is, in my flesh,) dwelleth no good thing: for to will is present with me; but *how* to perform that which is good I find not. Romans 7:18.

You do however, have the choice either to allow Satan to continue having the authority and influence over the web of your heart, (*leb*[15]), or you can elect to having that control relinquished by the authority of the codicil that has been levied against Adam's legacy. That codicil being divine grace provided for by God through the atoning blood of Jesus Christ. For if by one man's offence death reigned by one; much more they which receive abundance of grace and of the gift of righteousness shall reign in life by one, Jesus Christ.) 18 Therefore as by the offence of one *judgment came* upon all men to condemnation; even so by the righteousness of one *the free gift came* upon all men unto justification of life. 19 For as by one man's disobedience many were made sinners, so by the obedience of one shall many be made righteous. Romans 5:17-19. And almost all things are by the law purged with blood; and without shedding of blood is no remission. Hebrews 9:22.

To continue allowing satanic influence to deceive your heart, (*leb*[15]), is to be that seed that has fallen on the "wayside." The only way the "wayside" ground of the heart, (*leb*[15]), can be changed is to allow God to revoke the bequest that Adam's transgression has placed upon your soul, (*psuche*[40]). This can only be accomplished by the full repentance for the sinful state of your heart, (*leb*[15]), and soul, (*psuche*[40]), and accepting complete total responsibility for all sin, past, as well as present and current, that has ravaged the ground of the current status of your heart, (*leb*[15]). Then repenting for the commission of those sins, as well as any sins of omission, and acknowledging that the price for sin has been paid for by the blood of Jesus; then by accepting that blood as the paid price for your sin, then asking the Lord Jesus Christ to cleanse and to come into your heart, (*leb*[15]), is the only way the soul, (*psuche*[40]), is able to become weed (sin) free, and is the only way the soul, (*psuche*[40]), is able to stay weed (sin) free.

Doing so will turn the wayside, rocky, or thorny ground of the heart to that of good ground. The fertility of the ground of the soul, (*psuche*[40]), will then be regulated by the governing mandates that are issued from choices that are formulated in the heart, (*leb*[15]). You are then in control of the type of ground your life ultimately becomes as you: Draw nigh to God, and he will draw nigh to you. Cleanse *your* hands, *ye* sinners; and purify *your* hearts, *ye* double minded. 9 Be afflicted, and mourn, and weep: let your laughter be turned to mourning, and *your* joy to heaviness. 10 Humble yourselves in the sight of the Lord, and he shall lift you up. James 4:8-10. The state of the soul, (*psuche*[40]), be it rocky ground, thorny ground, or good ground will then be determined by the depth of the dedication, as well as the commitment and percent of surrender of the governing authority of the heart, (*leb*[15]), to the laws of God. However, the condition of that ground can and will change, for the better or the worse, depending on the allegiance to the master that your heart, (*leb*[15]), is committed to obeying, either to the law of righteousness or the lust of carnal depravity: No man can serve two masters: for either he will hate the one, and love the other; or else he will hold to the one, and despise the other. Ye cannot serve God and mammon. Matthew 6:24. The fertility of that ground will either increase with the increase of spiritual fervor, or will decrease with the increased consorting with carnality. The condition of the ground of the soul, (*psuche*[40]), will never remain in a neutral state.

Maybe after your soul, (*psuche*[40]), has been restored by the grace of God through the redemptive power of Calvary, and you have lost all appetite for the thorns and thistles, yet, you find you are still plagued with the effects that the thorns have scared your life with, as sin always leaves permanent scars. The accuser of the brethren will ever attempt to reopen those scars by intimidation as we walk the straight and narrow road: Enter ye in at the strait gate: for wide *is* the gate, and broad *is* the way, that leadeth to destruction, and many there be which go in thereat: 14 Because strait *is* the gate, and narrow *is* the way, which leadeth unto life, and few there be that find it. Matthew 7:13-14. The scarred effects of past forgiven sins hold no weight in divine jurisprudence: I write unto you, little children, because your sins are forgiven you for his (Jesus) name's sake. 1John 2:12. Once vindicated through divine jurisprudence, we are free and clear of all satanic charges that he will ever be able to level against us, as the Lord will not impute sin once it has been confessed and forgiven: *Saying*, Blessed *are* they whose iniquities are forgiven, and whose sins are covered. 8 Blessed *is* the man to whom the Lord will not impute sin. Romans 4:7-8. Satan will however, attempt to use the scared effects of those past sins as weapons against us in spiritual warfare that often rage against the soul. These things I have spoken unto you, that in me ye might have peace. In the world ye shall have tribulation: but be of good cheer; I have overcome the world. John 16:33

As long as this present world stands, we will never be able to be rid of the effects from the thorns and thistles of our past. But if the blood of Jesus Christ has cleansed and removed them from our heart, (*leb*[15]), then as we continue to walk in the light, the need to ever have to account for forgiven sins has also been removed from the record of our life as well: As far as the east is from the west, *so* far hath he removed our transgressions from us. Psalm 103:12. However, it is up to us as individuals to keep all thorns and thistles from re-infesting the ground of our heart, (*leb*[15]), thereby returning that good ground back to that of thorny, rocky, or even contaminated wayside ground. But when the righteous turneth away from his righteousness, and committeth iniquity, *and* doeth according to all the abominations that the wicked *man* doeth, shall he live? All his righteousness that he hath done shall not be mentioned: in his trespass that he hath trespassed, and in his sin that he hath sinned, in them shall he die. Ezekiel 18:24. Should one find themself again snared by sin, there is still hope for the penitent: Again, when the wicked *man* turneth away from his wickedness that he hath committed, and doeth that which is lawful and right, he shall save his soul alive. 28 Because he considereth, and turneth away from all his transgressions that he hath committed, he shall surely live, he shall not die. Ezekiel 18:27-28. God through the Lord Jesus Christ has made provisions for the penitent heart, (*leb*[15]). If we confess our sins, he is faithful and just to forgive us *our* sins, and to cleanse us from all unrighteousness. 1 John 1:9.

It may be that you have made dim-witted decisions or attempted a foolish endeavor that ended with catastrophic results involving the loss of health, time, finances or other resources. Perhaps you have helped someone to recover from a personal dilemma only to find yourself embroiled in a law suit that was caused by their shady dealings. You may have helped a friend with a business pursuit only to realize too late that you were used as a scapegoat that, that person used to bail themself out of a bad business venture. Maybe one of these or perhaps another issue has left you destitute and without any recourse for recovery. It may be that the only recompense you have been left with is the perpetual internal grinding of nerves that keeps gnawing within your heart, mind, body, soul and spirit leaving you destitute and robed of your peace and you find it difficult to commune or even to continue living for God. There is only one way full restoration can be made to your soul, (*psuche*[40]), and that is forgiving the offender(s) the same as God has forgiven you. The strength of this is when you sincerely forgive the offender(s) even without them asking for your forgiveness: And when ye stand praying, forgive, if ye have ought against any: that your Father also which is in heaven may forgive you your trespasses. 26 But if ye do not forgive, neither will your Father which is in heaven forgive your trespasses. Mark11:25-26. Even Christ on the cross cried out for the forgiveness of His offenders, which includes you and I: Then said Jesus, Father, forgive them; for they know not what they do. And they parted his raiment, and cast lots. Luke 23:34. I know from experience that this will not be easy. For years after being a recipient of God's mercy and grace, I carried hate, scorn, bitterness and contempt in my heart, (*leb*[15]), against many, including my entire family. It wasn't until after I finally forgave all, not some but all for the negative issues that had for whatever reason been lodged against me, that I found true peace. Forgiveness is a two-way street as forgiving without forgetting, is not forgiveness! True forgiveness then becomes a one way street as, I press toward the mark for the prize of the high calling of God in Christ Jesus. 15 Let us therefore, as many as be perfect, be thus minded: and if in any thing ye be otherwise minded, God shall reveal even this unto you. 16 Nevertheless, whereto we have already attained, let us walk by the same rule, let us mind the same thing. Philippians 3:14-16.

Possibly it has been that Satan has buffeted you with other issues, by infesting your mind with "you are not good enough," or "God doesn't care about you," or " you are too sinful," or " God can't or won't forgive that" etc. Possibly you are confronted with reoccurring accounts of a past sin, whose effects are continually terrorizing you with "your confession was only cold indifference of the mind, and not wholehearted repentance of the heart, (*leb*[15])," and the accuser is attempting to again flood your heart, *leb*[15], with a regrowth of thorns and thistles within your soul, (*psuche*[40]), that were caused by the effects of that sin. This is simply an attack on your faith: Now the just shall live by faith: but if *any man* draw back, my soul shall have no pleasure in him.

Hebrews 10:38. It is also a time to again thank God, not to confess, but to thank God again for redeeming your soul, *psuche*[40], from corruption and destruction: But this man, (Jesus) after he had offered one sacrifice for sins for ever, sat down on the right hand of God; 13 From henceforth expecting till his enemies be made his footstool. 14 For by one offering he hath perfected for ever them that are sanctified 15 *Whereof* the Holy Ghost also is a witness to us: for after that he had said before 16 This *is* the covenant that I will make with them after those days, saith the Lord, I will put my laws into their hearts, and in their minds will I write them; 17 And their sins and iniquities will I remember no more. 18 Now where remission of these *is, there is* no more offering for sin. Hebrews 10:12-18.

As long as this world stands, the earth will always be filled with thorns and thistles simply because Adam chose submission to the persuasion of satanic deceit, that had been enhanced by the visible evidence of there being no apparent change in Eve after she ate of the fruit, over obedience to the divine law of God, when he disobeyed the voice of God by eating of the forbidden fruit. It is therefore impossible for there to be an end of tragedies and calamities, (thorns and thistles) in this present life on both a global, regional, local, public and personal level. The act of disobedience by Adam was not an act of defiance, it was simply an act of insubordination to the commandment God gave to him that was to be a defense against the cunning wiles of satanic aggression, to which Adam ultimately yielded. Nevertheless, it was still disobedience to God's command, law, therefore it was still sin: Let no man say when he is tempted, I am tempted of God: for God cannot be tempted with evil, neither tempteth he any man: 14 But every man is tempted, when he is drawn away of his own lust, and enticed. 15 Then when lust hath conceived, it bringeth forth sin: and sin, when it is finished, bringeth forth death. 16 Do not err, my beloved brethren. James 1:13-16.

Some tragic events are caused by the effects of nature, others by the mistakes of man, while most personal tragedies are caused buy our own self infliction and or indulgence as it were with forbidden fruit. I have come to the realization that the majority of the cataclysmic weed growth we find ourselves embroiled in emanate from the verdict of bad choices, wrong roads traveled that have led to tragic dead ends, and most importantly by violating the conscience simply by ignoring or going contrary to that still small voice that was attempting to communicate to our mind from the heart, (*leb*[15]): And he said, Go forth, and stand upon the mount before the LORD. And, behold, the LORD passed by, and a great and strong wind rent the mountains, and brake in pieces the rocks before the LORD; *but* the LORD *was* not in the wind: and after the wind an earthquake; *but* the LORD *was* not in the earthquake: 12 And after the earthquake a fire; *but* the LORD *was* not in the fire: and after the fire a still small voice. 13 And it was *so,* when Elijah heard *it,* that he wrapped his face in his mantle, and went out, and stood in the entering in of the cave. And, behold, *there came* a voice unto him, and said, What doest thou here, Elijah? 1Kings 19:11-13. As with the prophet Elijah, God still attempts to deal with His people through that still small voice, the voice of the conscience. Unfortunately, we often try to respond to God's prompting of the conscience by trying to communicate with the wind, or by rummage through the aftermath of the earthquake, or by grieving over the total devastation of the fire before we come face to face with our folly, while the still small voice still continually tries to intercede on our behalf.

When calamities do befall us, from either the probable consequence of ignoring the voice of the conscience, or as the result of violating one or more of God's commands, we need to seriously examine ourselves to determine if the consequence of that ill-fated debacle did in fact emanate as the result of an odious argument that had been issued by the governance of our heart, (*leb*[15]), to become responsible for any tragedy arising out of either our failure to heed the voice of the conscience or our failure to yield obedience to the discipline of divine jurisprudence. If honest examination indeed finds we are the responsible, then instead of trying to justify our ill fated actions and groaning oh me, or why me, we need to confess that we are the reason for our becoming entangled again in those weeds of thorns and thistles, or even responsible for others who may have become entangled as a result of our negligence. Confession and repentance then becomes the necessary response needed to begin the rectification of the issue: If we say that we have no sin, we deceive ourselves, and the truth is not in us. 9 If we confess our sins, he is faithful and just to forgive us *our* sins, and to cleanse us from all unrighteousness. 10 If we say that we have not sinned, we make him a liar, and his word is not in us. 1 John 1:8-10. If and when we do repent and confess we have the assurance in that: For I will be merciful to their unrighteousness, and their sins and their iniquities will I remember no more. Hebrews 8:12.

In wrestling among the thorns and thistles of this world, pressure will often arise from some unexpected quarter browbeating your soul, (*psuche*[40]) attempting to destroy your faith by proclaiming that you are still guilty and again need to confess and repent of some past sin. This attack on the mind is arrogant defiant ignorance of the deceleration of the profit Isaiah: I, (God) *even* I, *am* he that blotteth out thy transgressions for mine own sake, and will not remember thy sins. Isaiah 43:25. In these desperate times of despair we can take courage that: *There is* therefore now no condemnation to them which are in Christ Jesus, who walk not after the flesh, but after the Spirit. Romans 8:1. Walking in the Spirit will always defy the government of the carnal flesh: So then they that are in the flesh cannot please God. Romans 8:8. The victory of walking in the spirit is: Now the just shall live by faith: but if *any man* draw back, my soul shall have no pleasure in him. Hebrews 10:38. The reason being that Because the carnal mind *is* enmity against God: for it is not subject to the law of God, neither indeed can be. Romans 8:7.

Many times I have found myself victimized by satanic insinuations with an onslaught of intimidations issuing from the thorns and thistles which I ignobly cultivated prior to surrendering to the acceptance of Calvary's grace of redemption through the atoning blood of Jesus. After many a struggle, especially as the result of satanic conflict, being left feeling that I am nothing but a dismal failure without any needful or useful purpose in life, I have had to realize I am totally unable to do anything about the ancient history of my past. Even in those times I have been assured that: According to *their* deeds, accordingly he will repay, fury to his adversaries, recompence to his enemies; to the islands he will repay recompence. 19 So shall they fear the name of the LORD from the west, and his glory from the rising of the sun. When the enemy shall come in like a flood, the Spirit of the LORD shall lift up a standard against him. Isaiah 59:18-19. Many times the Holy Spirit has had to remind me when I didn't want to forgive, and even refused to forgive myself, that I was in fact calling God a liar as And be ye kind one to another, tenderhearted, forgiving one another, even as God for Christ's sake hath forgiven you. Ephesians 4:32. True peace only comes through genuine forgiveness and acceptance of the fact that we are forgiven.

This has helped me at times on several occasions to stand firm in the faith and in the liberty of Christ. Stand fast therefore in the liberty wherewith Christ hath made us free, and be not entangled again with the yoke of bondage. Galatians 5:1 The report of one recent account being: several years ago I moved from another state to where I now reside. The house I am renting has an attached garage, equipped with an automatic door opener. This garage being small, nineteen feet in length by thirteen feet in width, is about par for rental property as this house was built for. The vehicle I drive is a pick up truck sixteen and three quarter feet long. This gives me only twenty seven inches of free space, or as a worm might say, "wiggle room." Over the years I have made many mistakes while parking within the confines of this small garage. On several occasions I simply forgot the tail gate was down, before I lowered the garage door. The unimpressive consequence of my illustrious actions effectively altered the original design of the overhead door's top panel, resulting in a customized modification of that panel, (customization by crunch). Other times I neglected the fact that I had an elongated load in the truck bed extending more then twenty seven inches beyond the tail gate of the truck, which again as the door came down, further customizing was made to the design of that same top panel, (additional customizing by crunch), which was caused by my negligence. After calling myself everything but an intelligent sane human being, I would make the necessary repairs so the door would operate properly, while doing my best to resist the intimidations and accusations that kept relentlessly mocking my mind over my negligent carelessness.

Many times after I made the last repair to the door panel, the still small voice of my conscience prompted me many times to get a parking curb (wheel stop), and to place it appropriately on the garage floor so that I would know when I was within the safe confines of the garage's turf. However, I simply ignored that advice to the shame of my own detriment.

Then, it finally happened! One Sunday night after church service I pulled into the garage, but not within its safe confines. Not being attentive as to how the truck was parked, I let the door down. The result of my inattentive negligence made repair to the again modified top panel impossible. After struggling with intimidation over my inadvertent action, and doing my best to keep from going into an overbearing tirade over my negligent carelessness. I simply disengaged the drive opener from the door in order to be able to close the door. With my policy of "if I break or damage anything I will either repair it, have it repaired, or replace it," and this time with the panel being beyond repair, I knew I simply had to replace it.

That night I struggled often to keep the onslaught of negative intimidations from infesting my mind. Not wanting any more thorns or thistles in my life, I simply reminded the torment that was ragging against me that The LORD *is* good, a strong hold in the day of trouble; and he knoweth them that trust in him. Nahum 1:7. Even though I didn't have peace in going to bed that night, I did have victory. Don't tell me you can't have victory without having peace, I know better! The next day, after struggling with the issue at times through the night, in witch I kept reminding myself that I was the benefactor as well as the beneficiary of my own negligent action, and that there was no one or nothing else to blame but me for the required necessity of having to replace the damaged panel. Accepting the guilt of causing the crisis, made the repair operation of replacing the panel a lot smoother then It otherwise would have been. During the repair process I still cringed over the harassed intimidation being lodged against my mind over my negligent carelessness.

After completing the repair I had a wonderful wave of peace to sweep over me and I was truly able to thank God for the His helping hand throughout the entire ordeal. Yes, after the repair I immediately went and bought a parking curb and placed it to where I knew that I would be within the safe confines of the garage when I parked. It was after this that, that still small voice reminded me of my repair or replace policy, and that I was responsible for the unauthorized modification of the door panel's original design. Yes this incident was indeed a blessing for which I still rejoice.

You may wonder how it is that I can rejoice over this situation. It is because I accept full responsibility for my action without trying to find a scapegoat to blame it on and realizing that any iniquity within me is of my own negligence with which God nor anyone or anything else has anything to do with. In fact, God has done all He could do to keep me free from the ravages of many of life's pending personal crisis. I it is up to me as well as to you dear pilgrim to: Let not sin therefore reign in your mortal body, that ye should obey it in the lusts there of. 13 Neither yield ye your members *as* instruments of unrighteousness unto sin: but yield yourselves unto God, as those that are alive from the dead, and your members as instruments of righteousness unto God. Romans 6:12-13.

You dear pilgrim as well as myself are the ones responsible the seeds of iniquity that usurp contemptible influence and control of our heart, (*leb*[15]), that have the potential to ultimately germinate into acts of sin if we by choice allow them to. We are also the ones responsible when the seeds of iniquity issuing from our heart, (*leb*[15]), that germinates into a growth of sin that becomes the cause of tragedy, catastrophe, affliction, distress, anguish, sorrow, grief, pain, torment or any other negative affect that is or has been imposed upon others and even upon ourselves. We are also the ones responsible for all damage inflicted upon life, limb and property of others as well as ourselves that emanate from the course of our thoughtless or careless actions. And the peace of God, which passeth all understanding, shall keep your hearts and minds through Christ Jesus. 8 Finally, brethren, whatsoever things are true, whatsoever things *are* honest, whatsoever things *are* just, whatsoever things *are* pure, whatsoever things *are* lovely, whatsoever things *are* of good report; if *there be* any virtue, and if *there be* any praise, think on these things. Philippians 4:7-8

Lucifer who became Satan, was the instigator of sin. Sin was then passed to Adam by satanic deception, who bequeathed sin to us for an inheritance, and which will be passed on through us to all future generations: For *there is* not a just man upon earth, that doeth good, and sinneth not. Ecclesiastes 7:20 Once stained by sin, purity can never be recovered by carnal enterprise: What *is* man, that he should be clean? and *he which is* born of a woman, that he should be righteous? Job 15:14. This question raised by Eliphaz the Temanite in an accusation against Job has been answered by the Apostle Paul: Not by works of righteousness which we have done, but according to his mercy he saved us, by the washing of regeneration, and renewing of the Holy Ghost; Titus 3:5. All calamities, disasters, tragedies, or catastrophes that plague, cripple, obliterate, mutilate, maim, destroy or annihilate friends, families, nations, and even ourselves, are only weeds issuing forth from the ground that has been cursed because of Adam's disobedience.

You dear pilgrim, as well as myself are responsible for all of our actions as well as for any detriment that has been caused as a result of those actions. However, life will be a lot more pleasant, and the calamities of life so much easier to cope with when we at least, maybe not gladly, but willingly, accept the responsibility for the actions stemming from our careless behavior, knowing that Jesus on Calvary's cross took full responsibility for our actions as well as our sin so that by His blood, provision could be and has been made that enables us to be, and to stay weed free. For he hath made him *to be* sin for us, who knew no sin; that we might be made the righteousness of God in him. 2 Corinthians 5:21. Even after being redeemed, iniquity will still attempt to sprout seeds of sin in our lives. These attempts will come from the onslaught of satanic temptations assaulting the government of our heart, (*leb*[15]): Blessed *is* the man that endureth temptation: for when he is tried, he shall receive the crown of life, which the Lord hath promised to them that love him.[13] Let no man say when he is tempted, I am tempted of God: for God cannot be tempted with evil, neither tempteth he any man: [14]But every man is tempted, when he is drawn away of his own lust, and enticed. [15]Then when lust hath conceived, it bringeth forth sin: and sin, when it is finished, bringeth forth death. [16]Do not err, my beloved brethren. James 1:12-16. However, should we, or when we again find that seeds of iniquity are germinating, or are attempting to germinate in our heart, (*leb*[15]), confession needs to be made in order for them to be removed before they become sin; For I will be merciful to their unrighteousness, and their sins and their iniquities will I remember no more. Hebrews 8:12.

I went by the field of the slothful, and by the vineyard of the man void of understanding; [31]And, lo, it was all grown over with thorns, *and* nettles had covered the face thereof, and the stone wall thereof was broken down. [32]Then I saw, *and* considered *it* well: I looked upon *it, and* received instruction. [33]*Yet* a little sleep, a little slumber, a little folding of the hands to sleep: [34]So shall thy poverty come as one that travelleth; and thy want as an armed man. Proverbs 24:30-34 The secret of being victorious in the fray of life is acknowledging our fault when we are guilty, then accepting the responsibility for the negative consequences that have been caused from the seeds of iniquity that have been sown from our heart, (*leb*[15]), that have germinated into an act of sin. This will be a hard pill to swallow, but will help make dealing with the consequences more palatable: And I heard a loud voice saying in heaven, Now is come salvation, and strength, and the kingdom of our God, and the power of his Christ: for the accuser of our brethren is cast down, which accused them before our God day and night. Revelation 12:10. When the accuser of the brethren tries to weave its web of deceit in your heart out of the hair of your head, Simply remind him: But if we walk in the light, as he is in the light, we have fellowship one with another, and the blood of Jesus Christ his Son cleanseth us from all sin. 1Jonn1:7

Man's inherent nature to sin is a legacy given to us by Adam: For as by one man's disobedience many were made sinners, so by the obedience of one shall many be made righteous. Romans 5:19. We cannot disannul that legacy of sin that has been bequeathed to us through Adam. However, a codicil to that bequeath is available: Surely he hath borne our griefs, and carried our sorrows: yet we did esteem him stricken, smitten of God, and afflicted. 5 But he *was* wounded for our transgressions, *he was* bruised for our iniquities: the chastisement of our peace *was* upon him; and with his stripes we are healed. 6 All we like sheep have gone astray; we have turned every one to his own way; and the LORD hath laid on him the iniquity of us all. Isaiah 53:4-6. With the original legacy of Adam being mandatory upon all souls, (*psuche*[40]), the codicil is not. It is conditional: Know ye not, that to whom ye yield yourselves servants to obey, his servants ye are to whom ye obey; whether of sin unto death, or of obedience unto righteousness? Romans 6:16.

The tenets of that codicil that has been issued to the world was given to Moses on Mount Sinai: 1. Thou shalt have no other gods before me. 2. Thou shalt not make any graven image. 3. Thou shalt not take the name of the Lord thy God in vain. 4. Remember the Sabbath day to keep it holy. 5. Honor thy father and thy mother. 6. Thou shalt not kill. 7. Thou shalt not commit adultery. 8. Thou shalt not steal. 9. Thou shalt not Bear false witness. 10. Thou shalt not covet: Exodus 20:3-17. That codicil is enforced by the blood of God Himself through the obedience of Jesus Christ who willingly chose to become sin for us who were dead in trespasses and sin: John to the seven churches which are in Asia: Grace *be* unto you, and peace, from him which is, and which was, and which is to come; and from the seven Spirits which are before his throne; 15 And from Jesus Christ, *who is* the faithful witness, *and* the first begotten of the dead, and the prince of the kings of the earth. Unto him that loved us, and washed us from our sins in his own blood. Revelation 1:4-5, see Figure 1.

We dear pilgrim, are able to, and it is up to us to keep our soul, (*psuche*[40]), clear and clean of all thorns and thistles by the provisions of that has been made through that codicil to Adams legacy, made possible by the blood of Calvary's Lamb, Jesus: My little children, these things write I unto you, that ye sin not. And if any man sin, we have an advocate with the Father, Jesus Christ the righteous: 2 And he is the propitiation for our sins: and not for ours only, but also for *the sins of* the whole world. 1 John 2:1-2. That codicil is effective only through the sacrificial offering of Jesus Christ: For where a testament *is,* there must also of necessity be the death of the testator. 17 For a testament *is* of force after men are dead: otherwise it is of no strength at all while the testator liveth. Hebrews 9:16-17.

When our body, (*nephesh*[12]), returns to dust, and our spirit, ruach[6], returns to God who gave it then the legality of that codicil will either be enforced or revoked according to the one we have authorized to occupy either the temple of our body, or the web of our heart, (*leb*[15]). Verily, verily, I say unto you, The hour is coming, and now is, when the dead shall hear the voice of the Son of God: and they that hear shall live. 26 For as the Father hath life in himself; so hath he given to the Son to have life in himself; 27 And hath given him authority to execute judgment also, because he is the Son of man. 28 Marvel not at this: for the hour is coming, in the which all that are in the graves shall hear his voice, 28 And shall come forth; they that have done good, unto the resurrection of life; and they that have done evil, unto the resurrection of damnation. John 5:25-29.

So your rebuttal is, how can you say, "man is responsible for the devastating calamities that plague this earth, as well as himself, as God Himself many times sent evil on the very ones whom He created?"

God did send an evil spirit between Abimelech and the men of Shechem as judgment for the treachery that was shown to the house of Jerubbaal. 24That the cruelty *done* to the threescore and ten sons of Jerubbaal might come, and their blood be laid upon Abimelech their brother, which slew them; and upon the men of Shechem, which aided him in the killing of his brethren. 57 And all the evil of the men of Shechem did God render upon their heads: and upon them came the curse of Jotham the son of Jerubbaal. Judges 9:24, 57.

God sent evil affliction upon King Saul for his disobedience to fully comply with the orders given to him to completely destroy the Amalekites: For rebellion *is as* the sin of witchcraft, and stubbornness *is as* iniquity and idolatry. Because thou hast rejected the word of the LORD, he hath also rejected thee from *being* king 1Samuel 15:23. And it came to pass, when the *evil* spirit from God was upon Saul, that David took an harp, and played with his hand: so Saul was refreshed, and was well, and the evil spirit departed from him. 1 Samuel 16:23

In the case concerning the issue of the widow of Zarephath's son. This was simply the fulfillment of the course of life and was not evil from God. It was simply the result of the appointed time for the body to return to dust after being separated from the soul, which was to be returned to God who gave it. It was simply the normal result of the bequest that had been given to man by Adam: And he cried unto the LORD, and said, O LORD my God, hast thou also brought evil upon the widow with whom I sojourn, by slaying her son? 1 Kings 17:20. This bequest had been in effect form all past generations, and will be effective to all succeeding generations: And as it is appointed unto men once to die, but after this the judgment: Hebrews 9:27.

Evil from God came as the result of Manasseh's failure to walk in the path of righteousness laid out before him by his father Hezekiah, in returning Israel back into idolatrous worship. His leadership ended with evil from the LORD for provoking Him to anger for seducing Israel to do more evil then the nations before them. Therefore thus saith the LORD God of Israel, Behold, I *am* bringing *such* evil upon Jerusalem and Judah, that whosoever heareth of it, both his ears shall tingle. 2 Kings 21:12.

Evil from God came upon the Israelites for their flagrant iniquitous disobedience of God's commandments which led them into the Babylonian captivity. After 70 years of exile in Babylon to reckon with the evil of their ways, the people failing to consider the cause of their enslavement, again after returning from captivity, returned back to their old ways of disobedience to God's commandments in the profaning of the Sabbath. Then

I contended with the nobles of Judah, and said unto them, What evil thing *is* this that ye do, and profane the sabbath day? 18 Did not your fathers thus, and did not our God bring all this evil upon us, and upon this city? yet ye bring more wrath upon Israel by profaning the sabbath. Nehemiah 13:17-18.

Evil from God came for the idolatrous worshiping of the pagan gods that Israel was supposed to have destroyed: And say, Hear ye the word of the LORD, O kings of Judah, and inhabitants of Jerusalem; Thus saith the LORD of hosts, the God of Israel; Behold, I will bring evil upon this place, the which whosoever heareth, his ears shall tingle. 4 Because they have forsaken me, and have estranged this place, and have burned incense in it unto other gods, whom neither they nor their fathers have known, nor the kings of Judah, and have filled this place with the blood of innocents; 5 They have built also the high places of Baal, to burn their sons with fire *for* burnt offerings unto Baal, which I commanded not, nor spake *it,* neither came *it* into my mind: 6 Therefore, behold, the days come, saith the LORD, that this place shall no more be called Tophet, nor The valley of the son of Hinnom, but The valley of slaughter. Jeremiah 19:3-6.

Again evil came because of Israel's hireling shepherds who only had concern for their own welfare while neglecting their duty of tending to the sheep: Therefore thus saith the LORD God of Israel against the pastors that feed my people; Ye have scattered my flock, and driven them away, and have not visited them: behold, I will visit upon you the evil of your doings, saith the LORD. Jeremiah 23:2.

Evil will come from a righteous God for provoking Him with the same wicked works that were perpetrated by previous generations, whose works brought judgment upon man for their iniquitous ways: Have ye forgotten the wickedness of your fathers, and the wickedness of the kings of Judah, and the wickedness of their wives, and your own wickedness, and the wickedness of your wives, which they have committed in the land of Judah, and in the streets of Jerusalem? 10 They are not humbled *even* unto this day, neither have they feared, nor walked in my law, nor in my statutes, that I set before you and before your fathers. 11 Therefore thus saith the LORD of hosts, the God of Israel; Behold, I will set my face against you for evil, and to cut off all Judah. Jeremiah 44:9-11.

So skeptics shall sneer and say why, how can a kind loving God permit such horrific acts of injustices? Really? How can a righteous holy God not permit judgment on all evil, wicked, deviant behavior that violates his commandments? For thou *art* not a God that hath pleasure in wickedness: neither shall evil dwell with thee. 5 The foolish shall not stand in thy sight: thou hatest all workers of iniquity. 6 Thou shalt destroy them that speak leasing: the LORD will abhor the bloody and deceitful man. Psalm 5:4-6. This is simply the issue of man justifying his iniquitous actions before a holy God that knows better.

If a soul wants to avoid the evil pronounced by God, God has made very clear the course of action we are to pursue to avoid judgment. Therefore also now, saith the LORD, turn ye *even* to me with all your heart, and with fasting, and with weeping, and with mourning: 13 And rend your heart, and not your garments, and turn unto the LORD your God: for he *is* gracious and merciful, slow to anger, and of great kindness, and repenteth him of the evil. 14 Who knoweth *if* he will return and repent, and leave a blessing behind him; *even* a meat offering and a drink offering unto the LORD your God? Joel 2:1214.

God does not take pleasure in the punishment of man for his acts of iniquity as is prescribed and demanded by divine jurisprudence. Therefore, O thou son of man, speak unto the house of Israel; Thus ye speak, saying, If our transgressions and our sins *be* upon us, and we pine away in them, how should we then live? 11 Say unto them, *As* I live, saith the Lord GOD, I have no pleasure in the death of the wicked; but that the wicked turn from his way and live: turn ye, turn ye from your evil ways; for why will ye die, O house of Israel? Ezekiel 33:10-11

God does have a desire and willingness to repent of His decreed determined intentions of executing divine judgment on the indited guilty, as with the case of

Nineveh. Who can tell *if* God will turn and repent, and turn away from his fierce anger, that we perish not? 10 And God saw their works, that they turned from their evil way; and God repented of the evil, that he had said that he would do unto them; and he did *it* not. Jonah 3:9-10.

It was man's own iniquitous actions that caused evil to be sent from God upon both the nations, Judah and Israel, because of the flagrant disobedience to God's commandments. God simply judged man according to the jurisprudence He set by= divine law for the violation of His divine commandments. God was not, and is not willing that any should perish: Have I any pleasure at all that the wicked should die? saith the Lord GOD: *and* not that he should return from his ways, and live? Ezekiel 18:23

Now you are going to tell me that God made wicked people for the intent to destroy them: The LORD hath made all *things* for himself: yea, even the wicked for the day of evil. Proverbs 16:4. This is the ongoing argument of predestionation, for which much debate and volumes have been published. This issue of predestination is not germane to this argument and will not be addressed. Needless to say, God can not, did not, has not nor will not create anything that is in violation of the purity of His holiness! To do so would place God in violation of His own holy nature and character, placing Him on the same level with sinful man. For they being ignorant of God's righteousness, and going about to establish their own righteousness, have not submitted themselves unto the righteousness of God. Romans 10:3. Who will have all men to be saved, and to come unto the knowledge of the truth. 5 For *there is* one God, and one mediator between God and men, the man Christ Jesus; 6 Who gave himself a ransom for all, to be testified in due time. 1 Timothy 2:4-6. For all, even includes those who are supposedly made for destruction. A holy God cannot create or make anything that is contrary to the purity of His divine holiness. People turn themselves into becoming wicked when they refuse or reject the holiness of God in favor of their own self righteousness. Predestination is an argument germinated from the seeds of iniquity.

It always has been and always will be man's violation of divine jurisprudence that incurs the wrath of a long suffering God. However, God's wrath will ultimately be executed in judgment upon the children of disobedience for their violation of divine law. The children of disobedience will incur that wrath upon themselves as per the decision of their own choice. That choice will ultimately lead them into being the victims of free morale agency which declares I AM GOD!

Let God be true, but every man a liar; as it is written, That thou mightiest be justified in thy sayings, and mightiest overcome when thou art judged. 5 But if our unrighteousness commend the righteousness of God, what shall we

say? *Is* **God unrighteous who taketh vengeance? (I speak as a man) 6 God forbid: for then how shall God judge the world?** Romans 3:4-6

Character is what you do, or allow when no one is around to observe your actions

ENDNOTES

1   lord - Yhovah;(Jehovah) Strong's number H3068: yeh-ho-vaw' (the) *self Existent* or eternal; *Jehovah*, Jewish national name of God: - Jehovah, the Lord.

2   God - Eloah; Strong's Number H433: a deity or the deity: - God

3   God - Eloheem; Strong's number H430: the plural form of H433; *gods* in the ordinary sense; but specifically used (in the plural thus, especially with the article) of the supreme *God*; occasionally applied by way of deference to *magistrates*; and sometimes as a superlative: - angels, X exceeding, God (gods) (-dess, -ly), X (very) great, judges, X mighty.

4   Notes: Schaeffer, F. (1972), Genesis in Space and Time, in The Complete Works of Francis Schaeffer (Vol 2), (Westchester, IL: Crossway Books, 1982), p9-10   http://www.creationmoments.com/radio/transcripts/beginning
https://creationmoments.com/?page_id_all=2&s=genesis%20in%20space%20and%20ti me

5   Lord - kurios; Strong's number G2962: From êõ?ñïò kuros (*supremacy*); *supreme* in authority, that is, (as noun) *controller*; by implication *Mr.* (as a respectful title): - God, Lord, master, Sir.

6   spirit - breath, Ruach; Strong's number 7307: From H7306; *wind*; by resemblance *breath*, that is, a sensible (or even violent) exhalation; figuratively *life, anger, unsubstantiality*; by extension a *region* of the sky; by resemblance *spirit*, but only of a rational being (including its expression and functions): - air, anger, blast, breath, X cool, courage, mind, X quarter, X side, spirit ([-ual]), tempest, X vain, ([whirl-]) wind (-y).

7   moved - Rachaph; Strong's number H7363: A primitive root; to *brood*; by implication to *be relaxed:* - flutter, move, shake.

8   image - tselem; Strong's number H6754: From an unused root meaning to *shade*; a *phantom*, that is, (figuratively) *illusion, resemblance*; hence a representative *figure*, especially an *idol:* - image, vain shew.

9   WORDsearch Bible software: Standard Reference Library, Chapter 1 The Creation IV. Day Six (Genesis 1:24-31) B. Man Created(vv.26,27)

10   Matthew Henry's Commentary on the Whole Bible: e-Sword Bible software, Genesis 1:26-28

11   https://answersingenesis.org/who-is-god/creator-god/man-the-image-of-god/

12   body - soul, nephesh; Strong's number H5315: From H5314; properly a *breathing* creature, that is, *animal* or (abstractly) *vitality*; used very widely in a

literal, accommodated or figurative sense (bodily or mental): - any, appetite, beast, body, breath, creature, X dead (-ly), desire, X [dis-] contented, X fish, ghost, + greedy, he, heart (-y), (hath, X jeopardy of) life (X in jeopardy), lust, man, me, mind, mortality, one, own, person, pleasure, (her-, him-, my-, thy-) self, them (your) -selves, + slay, soul, + tablet, they, thing, (X she) will, X would have it.

13   Matthew Henry Concise Bible Commentary: Wordsearch Bible software; Genesis 1:26-28 (Man Created in the Image of God).

14   heart - Lebab; Strong's number H3824: From H3823; the *heart* (as the most interior organ); used also like H3820: - + bethink themselves, breast, comfortably, courage, ([faint], [tender-] heart([-ed]), midst, mind, X unawares, understanding.

15   heart - leb; Strong's number H3820: A form of H3824; the *heart*; also used (figuratively) very widely for the feelings, the will and even the intellect; likewise for the *centre* of anything: - + care for, comfortably, consent, X considered, courag [-eous], friend [-ly], ([broken-], [hard-], [merry-], [stiff-], [stout-], double) heart ([-ed]), X heed, X I, kindly, midst, mind (-ed), X regard ([-ed)], X themselves, X unawares, understanding, X well, willingly, wisdom.

16   Keep - natsar; Strong's number H5341: A primitive root; to *guard*, in a good sense (to *protect, maintain, obey*, etc.) or a bad one (to *conceal*, etc.): - besieged, hidden thing, keep (-er, -ing), monument, observe, preserve (-r), subtil, watcher (-man).

17 Diligence - mishma; Strong's number H4929: From H8104; a *guard* (the man, the post, or the *prison*); figuratively a *deposit*; also (as observed) a *usage* (abstractly), or an *example* (concretely): - diligence, guard, office, prison, ward, watch.

18 Conscience - Easton's Bible Dictionary: Wordsearch Bible software

19 Conscience - Nelson's Compact Bible Dictionary page 145 by Ronald F. Youngblood, F.F. Bruce & R.K. Harrison © 2004 by Thomas Nelson Publishers

20 Joseph Sutcliffe old and new testament commentary: e-Sword Bible software; Genesis 1:26

21 Hwaker's poor man's commentary: e-Sword Bible software; Ezekiel 28:11-19

22 Ironside notes on Selected Books: e-Sword Bible software; Ezekiel 28:1-26

23 anointed - mimshach; Strong's number H4473: From H4886, in the sense of *expansion*; *outspread* (that is, with outstretched wings): - anointed.

24 iniquity - evel avel avlah olah olah; Strong's number H5766: From H5765; (moral) *evil:* - iniquity, perverseness, unjust (-ly), unrighteousness (-ly), wicked (-ness).

25 heart - kardia; Strong's nimber G2588: Prolonged from a primary kap kar (Latin *cor*, "heart"); the *heart*, that is, (figuratively) the *thoughts* or *feelings* (*mind*); also (by analogy) the *middle:* - (+ broken-) heart (-ed).

26 iniquity - aven; Strong's number H205: From an unused root perhaps meaning properly to pant

(hence to exert oneself, usually in vain; to come to *naught*); strictly *nothingness;* also *trouble, vanity, wickedness; specifically an idol:* - affliction, evil, false, idol, iniquity, mischief, mourners (-ing), naught, sorrow, unjust, unrighteous, vain, vanity, wicked (-ness.) Compare H369.

27   death - epithanatios; Strond's number G1935: From G1909 and G2288; doomed to death: - appointed to death

28   death - thanatos; Strong's number G2288: From G2384; (properly an adjective used as a noun) *death* (litterally or figuartively): - X deadly, (be . . .) death.

29   e-Sword The Complete Pulpit Commentary Job 1:6

30   e-Sword Joseph Benson Commentary Job 1:6

31   SwordSearcher John Gill's Exposition of the Entire Bible Job 1:6

32   SwordSearcher John Wesley's Notes on the Bible Job 1:6

33   die - muth; Strong's number H4191: A primitive root; to die (literally or figuratively); causatively to kill: - X at all, X crying, (be) dead (body, man, one), (put to, worthy of) death, destroy (-er), (cause to, be like to, must) die, kill, necro [-mancer], X must needs, slay, X surely, X very suddenly, X in [no] wise.

34   glory - kabod; Strong's number H3519: From H3513; properly weight; but only figuratively in a good sense, splendor or copiousness: - glorious (-ly), glory, honour (-able).

35   Shekinah - Nelson's Compact Bible Dictionary page 565 by Ronald F. Youngblood, F.F. Bruce & R.K. Harrison © 2004 by Thomas Nelson Publishers

36   Sin - Nelson's Compact Bible Dictionary page 576 by Ronald F. Youngblood, F.F. Bruce & R.K. Harrison © 2004 by Thomas Nelson Publishers

37   Sorrow - itstsabon; Strong's number H6093: From H6087; *worrisomeness*, that is, *labor* or *pain:* - sorrow, toil.

38   e-Sword - Adam Clarke's commentary on the Bible Genesis 8:21.

39   e-Sword - Pulpit Commentary Genesis 8:21.

40   soul - psuche; Strong's number G5590: From G5594; breath, that is, (by implication) spirit, abstractly or concretely (the animal sentient principle only; thus distinguished on the one hand from G4151, which is the rational and immortal soul; and on the other from G2323, which is mere vitality, even of plants: these terms thus exactly correspond respectively to the Hebrew [H5315], [H7307] and [H2416]: - heart (+ -ily), life, mind, soul, + us, + you.

41   atonement - katallage; Strong's number G2643: From G2644; exchange (figuratively adjustment), that is, restoration to (the divine) favor: - atonement, reconciliation (-ing).

42   pythons being responsible for decimating the Everglades   https://weather.com/news/news/201 8-09-02-hybrid-snake-burmese-python-everglades http://time.com/3752598/burmese-pythons-taking-over-everglades/ https://www.dw.com/en/the-burmese-python-and-the-fight-for-the-florida-everglades/a-44599606 http://animalstime.com/burmese-python-facts/ https://www.cbsnews.com/news/burmese-python-

invasive-species-in-florida-hurricane-andrew-legacy-cbsn-originals/ https://www.npr.org/2012/01/31/146124073/pythons-blamed-for-everglades-disappearing-animals

43   ground, earth - adamah; Strong's number H127: From H119; soil (from its general redness): - country, earth, ground, husband [-man] (-ry), land.

44   defile, destroy - phtheiro; Strong's number G5351: Probably strengthened from phthio (to pine or waste): properly to shrivel or wither, that is, to spoil (by any process) or (genitive) to ruin (especially figuratively by moral influences, to deprave): - corrupt (self), defile, destroy.